Gideon approached her with a bunch of yellow daisies and blue cornflowers. "Here." He shuffled his feet and handed her the flowers. "I thought you might like to put these on your mother's grave."

When she lifted her eyes to his face, the tenderness she saw there unsettled her. Other than Mama, she couldn't remember anyone ever defending her or extending kindness to her. She barely knew this man. Only his name: Gideon.

She accepted the wildflowers and mumbled a thank-you. Bowing her head, she closed her eyes so she wouldn't have to watch the body of her mother lowered into the hole. Oh, how she longed to feel the comfort of Mama's arms around her one more time.

She held the flowers to her face while the men filled in the grave. Then she sank to her knees and laid the flowers on the fresh mound. "Mama," she whispered through her tears. "What am I going to do without you?"

CONNIE STEVENS lives in north Georgia with her husband of over thirty-five years, John. She and John are active in a variety of capacities in their home church. One cantankerous kitty—misnamed Sweet Pea—allows them to live in her home. Some of Connie's favorite pastimes include reading, sewing, browsing antique shops, collecting teddy bears, and gardening. She also enjoys making quilts to send to the Cancer Treatment Center of America. Visit Connie's Web site and blog at www.conniestevenswrites.com.

Leave Me Never

Connie Stevens

Heartsong Presents

To my mother, from whom I inherited my love of books and storytelling. I miss you, Mom.

A note from the Author:
I love to hear from my readers! You may correspond with me by writing:

Connie Stevens
Author Relations
PO Box 721
Uhrichsville, OH 44683

ISBN 978-1-61626-017-0

LEAVE ME NEVER

Our mission is to publish and distribute inspirational products offering exceptional value and biblical encouragement to the masses.

PRINTED IN THE U.S.A.

one

Willow Creek, Iowa, 1881

Looking into Mama's face had always been like looking into a mirror, but not anymore. The skin on Mama's face hung over her cheekbones, creating gaunt hollows where beauty once resided. Tessa wiped her tears with the hem of her apron. For the first time in months, the lines between her mother's brows smoothed out. Her struggle was over.

"Mama." Tessa's own whisper echoed within the wagon canvas. "Oh Mama, please don't leave me here. Take me with you." Brokenness more cruel than anything she'd ever known invaded her heart with an onslaught so brutal she couldn't remember how to breathe. She straightened out her mother's fingers and laced them together in a posture of prayer, hoping against hope those fingers would squeeze hers once more. They didn't.

With leaden legs, Tessa slid to the end of the tailgate and lowered herself to the ground. Dawn had broken, but the morning mist still lingered over the unfamiliar town. Papa hadn't returned to their rickety wagon all night. Why wasn't he here? No doubt he drank himself blind again.

God, I need help. I don't know what to do.

She forced her eyes to scan her surroundings—for what, she wasn't sure. The edge of town where Papa left the wagon yesterday didn't offer much of a vantage point. A giant elm tree and thick underbrush offered meager privacy from the nearest building, the livery. Horses dozed in the corral, uninterested in her plight. The rest of the town seemed set apart, as though a line had been drawn in the dirt that she and her family weren't permitted to cross.

Farther down the street, a patchwork of brick and board buildings lined up like mourners in a funeral procession. An occasional sign, hitching rail, or picket fence broke the monotony of weathered storefronts, but the silent buildings offered no hint of the people residing within. Was there anybody in this town who could help her do what needed to be done?

Under different circumstances, she might consider this a pretty little town. She moved forward and crossed the space between the wagon and the corral, stopping at the watering trough in front of the livery. Her reflection in the still water startled her. A stranger—weary and disheveled—looked back at her. She dipped her cupped hands into the trough and lifted cool water to her face. With wet fingers she smoothed her hair. The cramped muscles in her back protested as she straightened to look down the street. Papa was nowhere to be seen.

Tessa's feet balked. Part of her heart was back in the wagon, stilled and unbreathing. Her constant source of unfailing love was now silent. Gentle, uncomplaining Carly Langford, her precious mama, would never call her "honey girl" again.

As she stood anchored in place by her grief, the gradual sights, smells, and sounds of a town awakening from slumber stretched their arms and yawned a greeting to the sun. Frying bacon and fresh-perked coffee wafted on the air. Then a rooster crowed. Strange sounds seeped into her awareness, and she realized it was birds chirping to each other in the trees. Eventually shopkeepers opened their doors to welcome the start of a new day. The comforting music of a town where everything was as it should be.

How could such cheerfulness exist? What was the matter with these people? Tessa wanted to scream for everyone to stop. Didn't they care that her mama just died?

"Miss?"

Tessa turned.

A tall, dark-haired young man stood behind her. His image wavered through her tears. "Miss, are you all right? Can I call somebody for you?"

She blinked back the tears and drew in the deepest breath she could manage. "A preacher. I need a preacher."

The stranger took her by the elbow and guided her to the board sidewalk. "Why don't you sit down here, miss? I'll go find the preacher and bring him. Can I get you anything?"

Tessa shook her head. The movement felt numbed and disconnected. As soon as she sat, the stranger strode away down the street. A slight breeze lifted the wisps of hair that lay along her cheek. "Oh God, I wanted to go with Mama. Why couldn't You take me, too?"

The rooster crowed again. A pair of little boys ran down the boardwalk, their laughter trailing strangely in their wake.

The wide doors of the livery opened, first one then the other. A wiry, whiskered man in a leather apron propped a rock in front of each door. He returned inside but reappeared a few moments later, dragging Papa by the arm. "Get on outta here. This ain't no hotel for drunks."

Papa stumbled over his feet, hitting the dust with a thud. His half-empty whiskey bottle broke on impact. Curses spewed from him as he got to his knees, contaminating the air with vile oaths. He squinted in her direction. "Tessa! Tessa, that you?"

Tessa squeezed her eyes shut, wishing she could block out the sound of her father's voice. Where was he when Mama needed him? "Yes, Papa, I'm here."

Papa staggered to his feet and kicked the remaining shards of broken glass. "What're you doin' just sittin' there, girl? Get me some breakfast."

A dull throb at the base of her skull caused Papa's demands to ring in her ears. "There is no breakfast, Papa. Nothing but the corn dodgers left from yesterday."

Storm clouds built behind her father's eyes. "Whadja say to me?" His voice slurred, and his watery, bloodshot eyes narrowed into slits. "You miserable little brat. How dare ya talk that way to your papa!"

He drew his hand back and slapped her across the face, sending her sprawling into the dirt. The metallic taste of blood touched her tongue, but she didn't care. Nothing Papa did mattered now. Her heart was numb.

Papa lurched over to where she lay in the dirt. He grabbed her arm and yanked her up then backhanded her again, knocking her backward against the livery door.

"Hey! Stop that!" The unfamiliar voice seeped through her daze. "What's the matter with you, mister?" The same stranger who told her he'd get the preacher stood before her. "Miss? Are you all right?"

She blinked and realized two men held Papa up by his arms and that another older man stood beside the dark-haired stranger.

"Are you all right, miss?" The older gentleman with thin, silver hair echoed the younger man as he bent to peer at her.

What difference did it make? "Yes, I'm all right."

"I'm Pastor Witherspoon. Gideon here says you need a preacher."

Gideon? Tessa slid her gaze to the tall young man. His dark scowl was fixed on Papa, but when he turned to look at Tessa, his eyes immediately softened into something foreign. Is that what sympathy looked like?

"Do you know that man?" His voice was low and even. The young man's finger pointed at Papa, who stood with splayed legs, swaying as though the breeze would blow him over.

"He's my father."

"Where is your mother, child?" Pastor Witherspoon touched Tessa's hand.

In order to answer the preacher, she would have to give voice to words she didn't want to speak. Loathsome, ugly words. But the preacher awaited her answer.

"Mama. . .Mama's in the wagon. She's. . ." Tessa couldn't allow the word to cross her lips, as though holding it back would erase the reality. If she didn't speak it, it simply wasn't so.

The man called Gideon strode across the yard in front of the livery to where the wagon sat partially concealed by low-hanging branches from the elm and drew aside the flap. He stepped up and leaned inside the canvas then exited slowly. "She's dead, Preacher."

"Dead!" Papa roared. "I told you!" He pointed his finger at Tessa. "This is your doin'. It's your fault. If it weren't for you, I'd still have a wife. You killed her, sure as I'm standin' here. Your mother's death is on your head, you no-good, miserable—"

"That's enough!" The dark-haired man drew back a fist.

Before he could throw the punch, the preacher grabbed his arm. "Gideon!" Pastor Witherspoon turned him away from Papa. "This young lady needs our help now, and her mother needs a Christian burial. Let's get busy and do what needs doing."

Gideon nodded, cast another withering glance at Tessa's father, and motioned to the livery man in the leather apron. "Cully, can you take him back behind the barn and let him sleep it off?"

"I ain't sleepin' now. I got things to do." The familiar belligerence of Papa's tone stung Tessa's ears. She knew better than to believe these men could change his mind.

Pastor Witherspoon stepped forward. "Sir, your wife's funeral is going to take place in just a little while. Why don't you go clean up and get some coffee, and when we're ready for the burial, you can—"

"I don't have time for no buryin'." He threw a glare at Tessa and pointed his chin at her. "*She* can do that. I got business." He shrugged off the men on either side of him. "Leave me alone. I got things to do."

He stalked down the street, leaving the small group staring after him.

All except Gideon. He looked at Tessa with such sympathy and compassion that she nearly lost control of what little resolve she had left.

She looked away and stiffened her spine. Papa would be drunk the rest of the day. It was up to her to see to it her mother was treated with the respect and caring she deserved. "Pastor, can you help me bury my mother?"

The elderly preacher took her hand and patted it. "Of course, child."

Gideon stepped forward. "I'll take care of it, Pastor. If you can look after Miss. . ."

"Langford," Tessa supplied. "Tessa Langford. My father is Doyle Langford, and Mama. . .Mama's name is Carly."

The preacher turned to Tessa. "Come with me, child. Mrs. Dunnigan at the boardinghouse will give you something to eat and a place to freshen up."

Tessa hesitated. "I have no money. I can't even pay for a decent burial for my mother."

Pastor Witherspoon waved his hand and nudged her ahead of him like the declaration of her poverty wasn't anything he hadn't heard before.

Two hours later, a small group stood around the freshly dug grave on a rise beyond the edge of town. A scattering of makeshift crosses and headstones dotted the grassy area where butterflies played tag among the wildflowers and cicadas provided the funeral music.

Mrs. Dunnigan from the boardinghouse stood beside

Tessa and patted her shoulder. Gideon and two other men, each holding his hat in one hand and a shovel in the other, stood opposite the mound of dirt. They listened while the preacher read from the Psalms.

Tessa thought it fitting that he read from Mama's favorite book of the Bible. She felt a brief wave of relief that Papa saw fit to stay away, but guilt immediately assaulted her for thinking so. Despite Papa's hateful words and drunkenness, something within her longed for his approval. Couldn't he see she'd tried her best to take care of Mama? He'd always blamed her for Mama's illness and told her she was a sorry substitute for the son Mama never had. Was she the reason he sought solace from a bottle?

After the preacher finished reading and praying, Gideon approached her with a bunch of yellow daisies and blue cornflowers. "Here." He shuffled his feet and handed her the flowers. "I thought you might like to put these on your mother's grave."

When she lifted her eyes to his face, the tenderness she saw there unsettled her. Other than Mama, she couldn't remember anyone ever defending her or extending kindness to her. She barely knew this man. Only his name: Gideon.

She accepted the wildflowers and mumbled a thank-you. Bowing her head, she closed her eyes so she wouldn't have to watch the body of her mother lowered into the hole. Oh, how she longed to feel the comfort of Mama's arms around her one more time.

She held the flowers to her face while the men filled in the grave. Then she sank to her knees and laid the flowers on the fresh mound. "Mama," she whispered through her tears. "What am I going to do without you?"

&

Gideon watched as Mrs. Dunnigan coaxed the poor girl away from her mother's grave and walked her back to the boardinghouse. With her father a drunk and her mother gone, what kind of life would she have now? She appeared to be close to his sister's age, and he hated to imagine Martha being left in such a depressing situation.

When he'd placed the bouquet of wildflowers in her hands, her fingers reminded him of the delicate bone china he sold in the mercantile. Her red-rimmed hazel eyes tore at his heart, and her wheat-colored hair escaped its sorry scrap of a ribbon and wisped in a dozen different directions. He was sure Mrs. Dunnigan would help her clean up, but what good would it do if she was destined to fetch and carry for a drunkard?

The image in his mind made him grateful he'd been able to keep the family business going after his father died two years ago. Running the mercantile might not be what he wanted to do, but at least he and Martha had a roof over their heads. Gideon sent a quick prayer heavenward to thank God his younger sister was about to be married in just a few months to a fine, godly man.

The sun was high in the sky by the time Gideon reached Maxwell's Mercantile. He unlocked the doors and propped them wide open to invite customers. If only opening the doors was all it took to bring in business. The reason for the recent decline in his sales clomped down the sidewalk at that very moment.

"Maxwell." Henry Kilgore puffed out his chest to display the ornate watch chain hanging from his vest pocket. The ever-present cigar stuck in his teeth made the man sound like he was trying to talk with his mouth full.

Gideon ignored the man and entered the store, pulling his dark blue apron from its hook as he passed the storeroom door. The last thing he needed right now was another visit from Kilgore.

"Maxwell, didn't you hear me?"

"I heard you, Kilgore. What do you want?" As if he didn't know.

"I was wondering if you'd given any consideration to my offer to take this place off your hands. You'll have to admit I've offered you a fair price. You don't really want to stand behind a counter waiting on people the rest of your life, do you? I thought you were a bright lad. You could do better than being nothing more than a shopkeeper. But maybe I was wrong."

Ire grabbed Gideon's gut at the implied insult, but he refused to give Kilgore the satisfaction of seeing the effect of his offensive remark. He picked up a feather duster and began flicking it over the glass jars lining the counter. "My father was nothing more than a shopkeeper, Kilgore, until you pressured him into an attack of apoplexy. He worked hard, earned an honest living, and managed to provide quite nicely for his family."

Kilgore threw his head back and guffawed. "You call this providing quite nicely? I don't see the customers beating down your door."

Gideon turned to confront the accuser standing in the middle of his store. "I think we both know why that is, Kilgore. Ever since you came to town a couple of years ago, you've been buying up as many businesses as you can get your hands on. Many of my longtime customers are now trading at your Willow Creek Emporium. I know you can't possibly be turning a profit from the prices you're charging there, especially since you have to pay someone to run the place for you."

Kilgore pulled a match from his vest pocket, struck it on the bottom of his boot, and lit his cigar. He puffed several times in rapid succession until the foul-smelling smoke caused Gideon to take a step backward.

"I don't need to make a profit. I'm making enough money from my other enterprises. I can afford to lower my prices for the fine citizens hereabouts."

Gideon snorted. "It's not the fine citizens you're concerned about, and we both know it. You think if you take enough business away from me, I'll be forced to sell out and then you can charge whatever prices you want. You don't just want to own Maxwell's Mercantile. You want to own the town. Well, let me tell you, Kilgore, if I ever plan to sell, it won't be to you, seeing as how you probably sent my father to a premature grave." Gideon jerked his head in the direction of the entrance. "There's the door. Use it."

Kilgore laughed, but no mirth filled the sound. "I'm a patient man. . .for now. In another few months you'll be singing a different tune." He withdrew the cigar from his mouth and flicked the ashes on the floor. "Don't wait too long, though, Maxwell. I make a practice of getting what I go after, and I just might lower my offer. Remember, I can buy and sell you ten times over if I want to." An arrogant smirk filled the man's face. He took a long draw on the cheroot and blew the smoke in Gideon's direction before sauntering toward the door.

Ordinarily Kilgore's barbs found their mark and Gideon chewed on the crust of the man's arrogance all day. But today was different. Maybe because the distracting picture of young Tessa Langford at her mother's grave stuck in his head.

two

Tessa fought her way through the grogginess. As she struggled to sit up, the ragged edges of sleep fell away, and she realized two things: It was daylight, and she didn't know where she was.

Needles of panic pricked her stomach. Her glance skittered around the simple furnishings in the room, from the clean, white curtain on the window to the closed door. Like pieces of a puzzle coming together, Tessa extracted a sense of time and place. She remembered now. That nice lady who ran the boardinghouse tried to get her to eat something and then invited her to lie down and rest.

Along with the understanding of her surroundings came the resurgence of grief. The ache blew through her like a searing hot prairie wind, and a sob escaped her tight throat.

She almost didn't hear the soft tap on the door. The boardinghouse lady poked her head in. The woman reminded Tessa of a schoolmarm with her severely pinned, iron-gray hair and creases around her eyes. Tessa guessed the woman either laughed a lot or frowned a lot.

"I thought I heard you crying, poor thing." The woman came into the room. Tessa's dress hung over her arm. "You were so exhausted I didn't have the heart to wake you last night for supper. You needed to sleep."

Last night? Supper? Bright sunlight streamed in the window.

The woman draped the dress across the foot of the bed. "I hope you don't mind, but I washed out your dress. There's fresh water in the pitcher, dear, and I saved you some breakfast."

Confusion fought with grief for first place in Tessa's mind.

"I'm sorry. I don't mean to be stupid, but what time is it?"

The woman lifted the dainty watch pinned to her bodice. "It's almost ten thirty. You take your time freshening up." A soft smile deepened the creases in her face as she turned to leave.

Tessa scrambled from the bed and realized she was wearing only her chemise. She snatched up the dress and held it in front of her. "Uh, Mrs. . . .uh, ma'am, how long have I been here?"

"I'm Pearl Dunnigan, dear. We met yesterday, but I don't blame you for not remembering. After the funeral, you swallowed a few sips of tea before you collapsed on that bed, and you've been asleep ever since."

Tessa gasped. Papa would be furious. Heedless of Mrs. Dunnigan standing there, she lowered the dress and stepped into it. "Mrs. Dunnigan, I'm so sorry. I had no right to stay here. I told the preacher I had no money—"

Mrs. Dunnigan held her hand up. "It's perfectly all right, dear. You needed a quiet place to rest. Now come and eat something."

"But my father will—"

The woman's expression changed from sunny to stormy in an instant. "Your father will just have to wait a few more minutes." She clucked her tongue. "His behavior yesterday was deplorable. And such vile language! Didn't even attend his own wife's funeral, and the way he treated you. . .tsk-tsk."

As if suddenly realizing her words might be offensive, the woman's cheeks turned bright pink. "Well, anyway, come eat some breakfast. I think there's still some apple butter left." She slipped out the door.

Tessa's fingers fumbled with the buttons down the front of her dress. She pulled on her shoes—Mama's shoes, actually. Mama told her to wear them a couple of months ago when her own were beyond repair. A simple pair of secondhand shoes, certainly not much to look at, but tangible proof of the footsteps Mama left for her to follow.

After a quick washing of her face and arms, she pulled her hair back and secured it with a frayed scrap of old ribbon. How might she excuse herself and hurry back to the wagon without appearing ungrateful? She couldn't, in good conscience, take advantage of Mrs. Dunnigan's generosity and accept food without paying for it.

She followed the heavenly mingled fragrances of coffee, bacon, and biscuits and found the kitchen.

Mrs. Dunnigan turned from the stove when Tessa entered. "Here, dear, you sit down while I pour you some coffee." She reached for the coffeepot. "How about some bacon and eggs?"

"Thank you, ma'am, but I'm not hungry." She regretted the lie. "You've been so kind. I just wish I could pay you for your trouble."

Mrs. Dunnigan set a mug of coffee in front of her. "You need to eat something, child."

Tessa took several tentative sips of the steaming brew. The aroma of breakfast made her stomach growl, but she set her jaw and stiffened her spine against the temptation. The overriding fear of her father's wrath bullied every other thought—her grief as well as her hunger—out of the way. Despite Mrs. Dunnigan's kindness, she couldn't linger at the woman's table.

She took one more sip of coffee and stood. "Thank you, ma'am, for everything. You've been more than kind, but Papa will be furious if he's had to wait for me."

Mrs. Dunnigan's eyebrows dipped in disagreement, but she simply nodded and patted Tessa's shoulder. "All right, dear. You take care now. And I'm so sorry about your mother."

The lump in Tessa's throat prevented her reply, so she forced a smile and returned the woman's nod. She slipped out the door and scurried down the boardwalk, past the livery to the giant elm tree at the edge of town where Papa left the wagon yesterday—or was it the day before?

She arrived at the place beneath the giant elm tree, but the only evidence of the wagon's presence was the trunk Tessa shared with her mother, Mama's treasured hand-carved cabinet, and a crate containing a crude assortment of household items strewed in the bushes.

Tessa's feet froze in place as she stared at the belongings littering the ground. Beside them, a set of wagon tracks led away from town in a westerly direction. She forced her eyes to cast a wide search of the area. Reality laughed in her face. Papa dumped everything he didn't want or need off the tailgate and left without her. He'd discarded her like a piece of unwanted baggage.

She sank down in the dirt beside the trunk. Her mother's cabinet lay sideways in front of her, one door askew. A cracked teacup, a broken crock, Mama's apron—evidences of a meager existence, tossed aside in the dust. Tessa picked up each item by turn, wiped it clean, and cradled it in her lap. Papa may have viewed these things as worthless and unnecessary, but they belonged to Mama. They were priceless.

She employed some muscle and set the cabinet upright, noticing that the collision with the ground had broken one of the hinges. How could Papa treat Mama's cherished cabinet with such carelessness?

Placing each item exactly as Mama kept them in the cabinet, she let her hand linger on each one. Caring for her mother's things was a privilege.

When she opened the opposite cabinet door, she saw Mama's Bible wedged into one corner. She withdrew it and traced the edge of the worn leather cover with her finger. Mama taught her to believe and pray from the time she was a young child, but a troubling thought now clouded her mind. Mama always said God would never forsake them. Yet here she sat, in a barren patch of dirt, with nothing more than a handful of belongings and a bewildered heart full of memories. Was this the way God cared for His children? Leaving them alone in the midst of strangers?

She pressed the Bible against her chest. "Mama, I miss you so much. Papa's left me, too. I wish you could tell me what to do."

The tears she'd held back for the last two days finally released as her grief and fear sought expression. She fell on her face beside the cabinet, clinging to the Bible and sobbing into Mama's apron. The surrounding trees and underbrush afforded enough privacy to erase any fear of onlookers, and she no longer cared to control the emotions she'd kept hidden far too long.

By the time her sorrow was spent, her eyes burned and raspiness grated her throat. She lay on the ground hugging the Bible and apron for a time. There was no hurry. She had no place to go. Perhaps if she stayed right here, God might decide to reach down and take her, too.

≥≥

After an undetermined time, Tessa pulled herself to a sitting position and leaned against the trunk. If wishes could undo circumstances, she'd wish enough to erase her entire life, but whims didn't affect reality. She could choose to sit under this elm tree and die, or she could choose to survive.

The memory of Mama's voice whispering encouragement and telling her how precious she was despite Papa's tirades invaded her heart. Mama didn't choose to die. She didn't give up. She gave out, but not until she'd fought as hard as she could. Tessa could do no less.

Carefully brushing the dirt from Mama's Bible, she returned it to the cabinet and tucked the apron into the trunk. She dug past the few articles of worn clothing and located a small leather pouch buried at the bottom of the trunk. It contained a few coins Mama managed to keep hidden from Papa. Tessa untied the strings and dumped the contents into her hand. A pitiful amount of money, but it was enough to buy a handful of crackers and a bit of cheese.

Tessa rose and brushed off her skirt. She walked to the livery watering trough where she dashed some water in her face and smoothed her hair. After she retied the old ribbon holding her hair away from her face, she headed down the street looking for a general store.

She passed a half dozen buildings, some freshly painted, others weatherworn, until she came to Maxwell's Mercantile. The place looked similar to the store where she and Mama traded back home. The brick front encased a large window displaying assorted kitchenware and household items. Barrels of apples, milk cans, and brooms lined the boardwalk outside. A neatly lettered sign proclaiming the store's name hung overhead. Double doors with slightly chipped green paint stood open in a friendly invitation.

She stepped inside. The storekeeper, his back turned, measured coffee beans into the large grinder behind the counter. Two ladies chatted as they examined yard goods. Nobody noticed her, so she wandered through the store and sniffed the aroma of freshly ground coffee. The storekeeper spoke to his customers, but Tessa paid no attention as she fingered the cuff of a blue calico dress hanging next to a small display of bonnets.

"May I help you?"

Tessa jumped at the nearness of the voice, spun around, and came face-to-face with the man who'd handed her the wildflowers yesterday. Surprise registered on the man's face as well. What was his name? Her mind was too muddled to think.

"Your name's Tessa, isn't it?"

Tessa nodded. She forced words past her lips. "Yes, sir."

A wide smile filled his face. "It's Gideon. What can I get for you today, Tessa?"

Tessa reached into her skirt pocket and extracted a nickel. "Is this enough to buy some crackers and cheese?"

Gideon's gaze traveled to the coin in her hand. His eyebrows lifted, and Tessa could only guess what he must be thinking. He crossed to the counter and pulled layers of cheesecloth away from a large, waxed round of cheese. With a deft motion, he cut a generous wedge, too generous to cost only five cents. He wrapped the cheese in paper then scooped a handful of crackers into a paper bag. "Here you go." Gideon slid her purchase across the counter.

She laid her nickel beside the paper-wrapped cheese. "Thank you."

"I want to extend my condolences again for the loss of your mother."

The tears that consumed her earlier threatened again. She pressed her lips together and drew in a tight breath to deny any show of emotion in this public place.

Another customer entered the store, and Gideon greeted the woman politely. He glanced about the store. "Is your father with you?"

The mere mention of Papa set her stomach spinning. Fear and grief collided in her chest. Should she tell Gideon her father had up and left her? What kind of explanation could she give? That she was worthless and her father had no use for her? That she was alone and had no idea how she was going to survive? "No, he must have had something else to do."

"So where are you folks from, and where are you headed?"

She wasn't headed anywhere—now. Harsh truth accosted her, but courtesy required she answer Gideon. "Papa had a farm back in Indiana. But he didn't like being a farmer."

"Indiana, huh? Good farm country there. Why didn't your pa want to farm?"

"Work was too hard, I guess. He raised hogs and grew corn, but he said he couldn't make enough money to keep body and soul together."

Gideon nodded like he understood. "Farming isn't easy, and that's a fact. Your crop can depend on a lot of things—weather, insects, blight. Anything can turn a harvest sour no matter how hard a man works."

Tessa felt heat crawling up her neck. Papa failed to turn a decent profit because he drank more than he worked the fields or cared for the pigs. He'd charged her with the animals' care and railed at her when the porkers brought a lower than expected price. How could she tell Gideon the embarrassing truth?

"Has your pa come west to try farming here in Iowa?"

She didn't know why Gideon was interested, but she didn't wish to be rude. "Papa heard some men talking about gold strikes in the Black Hills country. He figured he could get rich if we went there and dug for gold."

Gideon's brows dipped into a V. "A few folks pulled some gold out of there several years back, but not many got rich. There's been no report of gold strikes up there for a long time. Maybe the man at the land office can give your pa information about farmland hereabouts. Lots of farmers here in Iowa have harvested bountiful crops of corn and wheat, and for the past several years, there's been a lot of farmers raising porkers and cattle, too. Your pa could do well here."

If Papa could've stayed away from the bottle long enough to devote time and energy to their farm, they'd still be in Indiana. Maybe Mama would still be alive. Instead he'd decided to chase a harebrained dream of getting rich, while putting Mama through the rigors of traveling to goldfields that were nothing more than a mirage. Tears burned their way to the surface and spilled over. Her throat convulsed when she tried to swallow back the sobs.

Gideon's eyes widened, and his brow furrowed. "I'm sorry, Tessa. I didn't mean to—"

Tessa didn't wait to hear any more. She ran out the door, mortified at her lack of control in front of Gideon.

She picked up her skirts and escaped back to the seclusion of the elm tree and dropped down beside the trunk, her chest heaving more from anger at Papa and shame over her tears than from running. At least she didn't have to admit Papa had abandoned her. If Gideon knew what a worthless person she was, he likely wouldn't be so kind to her.

Despite her humiliation, her stomach still complained of its emptiness. She unwrapped the hunk of cheese and broke off a few small bits. It wouldn't do to eat too much. The cheese and crackers would have to feed her for a few days, at least until she could find employment.

She nibbled slowly to stretch out her mealtime as long as possible. She closed her eyes and imagined the fragrance of warm yeast bread fresh from the oven and savory roast beef with tender potatoes and carrots. If she played this game of imagination each time she ate a bit of cracker or cheese, her mind might convince her she wasn't as hungry as she thought.

The lengthening afternoon shadows indicated there wasn't much daylight left. She couldn't impose on Mrs. Dunnigan again. The canopy of branches overhead would be her roof tonight, and the underbrush would serve as her walls.

Dread washed over her at the prospect of spending the night outside and alone, at the mercy of whomever and whatever might be lurking in the darkness. But if Mama was right, God would spend the night with her.

three

Tessa grunted as she pushed Mama's cabinet between the fat tree trunk and a scraggly juniper. Tangled underbrush snagged her sleeve as she dragged the crate across a patch of thorny weeds. The heavier trunk required all her strength to shove into a position where the shadows of the big tree and the thick juniper and yew bushes concealed it from anyone who happened by.

Straightening, she scrutinized her hiding place. Anyone milling around the livery at the edge of town was unlikely to see her through the brush. It was the best she could do.

The descending sun marked the signal for most of the businesses in town to close their doors. Most, but not all. Down the main street at the center of town, the Willow Creek Hotel with its fine brick facade attracted a steady stream of people coming and going.

Boisterous clamor increased at the saloon. A shudder rippled through her when she imagined the amount of whiskey consumed there each night and its effect on the families of the men who patronized the place.

Tessa wrapped the remains of her dinner in the store paper. When she opened the door of Mama's cabinet to tuck her provisions into a safe place, the Bible she'd hugged earlier begged to be picked up. Why, she didn't know. What could God possibly have to say to her? Still, perhaps reading the same words Mama read might offer comfort.

She extracted a tattered quilt pieced from flour sack scraps from the trunk and arranged a makeshift pallet under the broad limbs of the elm. She peered around the juniper boughs, searching for signs of snakes then made herself as comfortable as possible and opened the Bible. The waning light fell on the pages of the Psalms. Mama's favorites were dog-eared and underlined. Extra marks by the verses of Psalm 27 indicated Mama found solace in them.

With the book positioned to use all the light available, she began to read what her mother found comforting. One verse spoke of hiding her in the time of trouble. Did that mean God would conceal her from prying eyes during the night? She read another verse.

"Leave me not, neither forsake me, O God of my salvation."

Was God aware that she was alone and frightened, hiding in the bushes like some kind of animal? Did He know about the fear knotting her stomach as the noise from the saloon built to a raucous din? In the dim glow of the final ray of light, she held up the book and squinted at the next verse.

"When my father and my mother forsake me, then the Lord will take me up."

The Bible slipped from her grasp and fell to her lap. Mama always said God kept His promises. If that verse was a promise, it surely wasn't meant for her. Only people worthy of God's love received His favor, and Papa always said she "wasn't worth nothin'."

&

The morning sun fell across the ledger as Gideon added up the last column one more time. He totaled up the net profits and frowned at the number. The grim number remained the same no matter how many times he reworked the figures. Every month since Kilgore bought the Willow Creek Emporium, that number shrank a bit more.

He blew out a noisy sigh and slammed the journal shut. The bell on the front door jingled, and Gideon looked up to see the preacher entering the store. "Hello, Pastor Witherspoon. What can I get for you today?"

"Morning, Gideon." The silver-headed pastor handed Gideon a scrap of paper. "Here's my wife's list. How's business?"

"Well, Pastor, things are getting a little tighter all the time."

Fatherly concern deepened the lines around the preacher's eyes. "That a fact? Does this have anything to do with Henry Kilgore taking over the Emporium?"

Gideon pulled two cans of applesauce from the shelf and set them on the counter before pausing to look at the preacher. "I know every man has a right to make a living." He ran his fingers through his hair. "Kilgore is undercutting my price on just about everything. I understand that times are tough. If folks can save a few cents by going to the Emporium, I don't suppose I can blame them." He heaved a deep sigh. "But, Pastor, he's pulling so many of my regular customers away from me, I don't know how much longer I'll be able to stay in business. And I've cut my own prices to the bare minimum."

Gideon cast a glance toward the boardwalk and lowered his voice. "For the past two years, Kilgore's been buying up businesses all over town. He owns the hotel and, of course, his saloons, the newspaper, the tannery, even seven or eight of the farms around here. He practically forced Mr. Lee to sell the Emporium last year. Cully told me Kilgore is trying to buy the livery. Why?"

The preacher frowned. "I can't understand why Kilgore is doing this. Besides the Emporium, seems like he owns half the town now, and I hear tell he's trying to buy the bank."

"The bank? Can he do that?"

Pastor Witherspoon scratched his head. "I suppose, if he's got enough money."

"No doubt about him having enough money." Gideon resumed filling the preacher's order. "He wants to buy me out."

"What? Gideon, you mustn't sell. If Kilgore gets control of

this place, he'll fix prices and we'll all be at his mercy."

"I know that, Preacher. The fact is, my dream is to sell this place and start a horse breeding farm. I've been looking at some land, and I've sent out some inquiries about purchasing breeding stock." Gideon placed a box of lucifers beside the pastor's accumulated order and paused to search the kindly older man's face. "Pastor, I want to sell the mercantile to anybody but Kilgore, but his is the only offer I've gotten."

The preacher rubbed his chin. "I'll surely pray about this. You can count on that."

The bell on the door drew their attention as Tessa Langford walked into the store. Her faded green dress was clean, and her hair was neatly wound and pinned into a bun. When he smiled at her, she looked at the floor and twisted her fingers.

"Hello, Tessa. It's nice to see you again."

"Hello. . .Gideon. Hello, Pastor Witherspoon." Her voice was so soft Gideon barely caught her response.

"Tessa." The preacher smiled at her. "I heard you and your father had already pulled out. I guess I was mistaken."

Tessa's chin lifted a tad, and she straightened her shoulders. "No, Pastor, you weren't mistaken. I think Papa left yesterday morning."

Gideon and the preacher traded looks, and Pastor Witherspoon's brow furrowed. "What do you mean, you think he left? Are you saying that you didn't know he was leaving?"

Tessa blinked several times while her chin quivered, but she simply shook her head. "No, I didn't." She turned to Gideon. "I wondered if there might be a position available here at the mercantile. I am in need of employment."

Anger rushed through Gideon. He didn't understand the malice with which Tessa's father lashed out at her and could only attribute it to the man's drunkenness, but what kind of a father abandoned his daughter? He swallowed back the remark he wanted to make.

"Tessa, do you have a place to live?"

She dropped her gaze again. "Well, yes I do, sort of."

Pastor Witherspoon put his hand on Tessa's shoulder. "Child, you aren't old enough to be living on your own."

The tiniest hint of a half smile tilted one corner of her mouth. "I'm nineteen." She looked back at Gideon. "I'm old enough to take care of myself. All I need is a job."

Indignation filled Gideon's chest. Here she was, the same age as his sister who was engaged to be married. But Martha had a big brother to look out for her until her wedding day. Tessa had no one.

Her attempt to appear strong and composed was evident, unlike yesterday when her tears couldn't be hidden. An inclination to protect this young woman filled him. He didn't understand such feelings, knowing her only a few days. Someone certainly should be looking after her, but regardless of any willingness on his part, it didn't change the facts.

"I'm so sorry, Tessa. I'm sorry your father went off and left you, and I'm especially sorry that I can't hire you. I wish I could."

"I wish I could."

Tessa smiled. How she managed to smile in her position, he didn't know, but it endeared her to him. She thanked him and bid the preacher good-bye and walked out the door. When she stepped onto the boardwalk, however, Gideon noticed her shoulders slump. Oh, how he hated being the cause of her disappointment. He watched her walk across the street and wondered how many more places would turn her away.

⚬

Tessa stared at the ornate decor in the hotel lobby while she waited for the clerk to finish checking in a gentleman. The room was fancier than anything she'd ever seen. Polished wood paneling and molding set off maroon and ivory wallpaper with gold filigrees. A crystal chandelier matched the sparkling wall sconces. Even the clerk behind the marble-topped desk wore a black linen coat and necktie.

When the transaction was completed, Tessa stepped forward.

The clerk, a middle-aged man with thin hair and a thick belly, swept a lecherous gaze over her from head to toe. "Well now, what can I do for you?" He arched one eyebrow. The corner of his mouth twitched in a salacious smile.

Tessa didn't like the way he looked at her, but her need for a job pushed her uneasiness aside. "I'm looking for employment, sir. I can do just about anything. I can scrub and make beds, do laundry and—"

"Just about anything, huh? Well, Willow Creek can use some new talent." His chuckle sounded purely evil. "But you're in the wrong place, darlin'. You need to go over to the Blue Goose."

"Blue Goose? What's that?"

The man threw back his head and belly laughed, slapping his thigh. "The Blue Goose Saloon. It's down the street a ways. Some fancy feathers and a little paint, not to mention getting you out of that flour sack dress, and you might be a real welcome addition to the stable down there."

When Tessa understood his suggestion, she sucked in a sharp breath. Her face flamed with indignation. "Sir, that's not the kind of employment I'm seeking."

She spun and nearly collided with a portly gentleman with an unlit cigar sticking out of his teeth.

"Excuse me. . . ." She attempted to step around the man, but he caught her arm.

"Whoa, not so fast there, young lady." The cigar waggled up and down as he spoke, and she didn't know how he managed to keep it from falling out of his mouth.

"My name's Kilgore. I own this place. I heard you tell my

clerk you need a job. Why don't we go sit over here and talk?"

Hope sprang up in Tessa's heart. She resisted glaring at the desk clerk and followed Mr. Kilgore through an arched doorway to a table in the corner of the hotel dining room. The same wallpaper that adorned the lobby covered the walls in this room. Fancy tapestry drapes embellished the windows, and the tables boasted fine linens and crystal glassware.

He held the maroon tapestry-covered chair for her and called to the waitress to bring two cups of tea. After he lowered himself to the chair opposite her, he interlaced his fingers and tapped his thumbs together. "Now, young lady, tell me about yourself."

Tessa swallowed hard and fingered the edge of the ivory damask tablecloth. "I'm Tessa Langford. I can clean, do laundry, and cook. I'm good with sums, and I'm sure I could learn any job quickly." The waitress arrived with the tea, and Tessa took the opportunity to smooth her faded dress.

Mr. Kilgore stirred sugar into his cup and sat back in his chair looking her up and down in the same manner as the desk clerk. "Have you ever waited tables?"

"No sir, but I'm sure I can learn."

"You'd have to be friendly with the customers. The friendlier you are, the more they buy. If they like you, they might stick around for. . .other services."

Confusion churned in her stomach. She glanced around the room. "I'm certain I can learn to wait tables, but I don't understand what other services you mean."

Mr. Kilgore removed his cigar and took a sip of tea. "Don't be coy, Miss Langford. I'm not talking about waiting tables here in the hotel. You're better suited to my other establishments. I own the two best saloons in town, the Gilded Lily and the Blue Goose. I'm always looking to hire fresh young women who know how to satisfy my clientele. The right girl can make good money. Of course, I take my cut, but you could do well."

Tessa shot a glance through the archway to the hotel lobby. The desk clerk leaned forward on his elbows and watched her with a nauseating grin. She wanted to slap the faces of both men. Maybe Papa was right; the kind of degrading employment Mr. Kilgore was offering her was the best she could do, but honoring Mama's memory prevailed. She'd rather starve than serve whiskey to men like Papa. She pushed her teacup away and stood. "I'm sorry, Mr. Kilgore, but I'm not looking for that kind of work."

Before she could take a step, the man motioned for her to sit down. She didn't sit but waited to hear if anything he had to say resembled an apology.

"All right, maybe you think this is a Sunday school picnic and you're one of those people who thinks they're better than anybody else. That's fine, if you want to be pigheaded. I'm telling you, you could do a lot better, but if that's what you want, I can use someone else here in the kitchen and dining room. Thirty-five cents a day."

Tessa lifted her chin. "I need a place to stay, and I can't pay rent on thirty-five cents a day."

Kilgore scoffed. "I suppose you expect me to put you up in the grand suite?"

She stood her ground without blinking.

"Sassy little thing, aren't you? All right, there's a shed out back you can stay in, and I won't charge you rent. But I have to warn you—the tips you'll get here aren't even close to what you'd make at my other establishments."

Tessa remained standing. "Working in the kitchen and waiting tables in the dining room is just fine with me."

Kilgore stood and looked her over again, then he called the waitress over. "Tillie, take Miss Langford here to the kitchen, and tell Flossie she's the new worker."

As Tessa turned to follow the girl, Kilgore called after her.

"You think about what I said, and let me know if you change your mind."

She paused and half turned. "I thank you for this job, Mr. Kilgore, but I won't change my mind."

The man hooked a thumb under his suspender and snorted. "Suit yourself."

❧

The woman named Flossie stirred a large pot of thick stew while she studied Tessa. With her free hand, she pushed back drab brown hair that had escaped its loose bun. Crow's-feet framed her eyes. Suspicion steeled her gaze into a defensive wall. "Old man Kilgore might've said you was hired, but I ain't gonna train anyone to take over my job."

The cook's declaration took Tessa aback. "Oh no, ma'am, I'm not here to take anyone's job. It's my understanding I'm supposed to work *with* you."

The waitress, Tillie, crossed the kitchen. "Flossie, you keep askin' how Kilgore expects us to do everything. Maybe she's just here to help, like she says." She took biscuits from the warming oven and added them to her tray. "Give her a chance."

"Flossie, that's all I want—a chance."

The cook grumbled under her breath and turned her back to Tessa. "There's an apron on the hook in the corner. You can get started scrubbin' those pots. Don't have to show you how to scrub pots, do I?"

"No, ma'am."

"Ma'am? Nobody calls me ma'am."

Tessa poured hot water from the reservoir on the side of the huge stove into a bucket. "My mama taught me to show respect when I meet new people."

Flossie just grunted and continued stirring. "Don't know that you're strong enough to be of much help. You're a scrawny little thing."

Tessa didn't look up as she scrubbed a greasy pot. Arguing wouldn't convince Flossie. She'd need to pray for an opportunity to prove herself to the woman.

Pray? She supposed she should pray, but it was hard enough just reading Mama's Bible. If she asked for help, would God listen?

four

Tessa hung her apron on the peg and glanced once more across the spotless kitchen. Her raw hands stung, and her feet ached, but she had a job. Her body begged for rest, but she needed to go back to the elm tree and gather her belongings before she found Mr. Kilgore's shed.

She tried not to think about the fact she'd be living in a shed. Even without having laid eyes on the place, she presumed it wouldn't be more than a shack—probably unlivable when the cold weather arrived, if Iowa winters were as cold as Indiana winters. If she was frugal with her earnings for four or five months, surely she'd be able to save enough to afford a small room at Mrs. Dunnigan's place, at least for the winter.

She stepped out the side door into the alley. Lengthening shadows lined her way as she hurried down the street. The heightening noise from the saloons carried on the evening air, piquing her uneasiness. Drunken men always meant trouble.

As she passed Maxwell's Mercantile, the door opened and Gideon exited. When he looked up, recognition lit his eyes. "Tessa, good evening. I hope you had some luck finding a job." The same apologetic tone he'd used earlier colored his voice.

"I did, thank you. I'm working at the hotel."

Even in the deepening shadows, she saw him scowl. "You're working for Kilgore?"

"Yes." No sense humiliating herself by telling him of Kilgore's first offer. "I'm working in the kitchen and dining room. If you'll excuse me, I'm very tired, and I still have to move my things."

"Your things?"

"Yes. Mr. Kilgore was kind enough to give me a place to stay behind the hotel. I need to move my belongings there."

When she started around him, Gideon stopped her. "Please, allow me to help. I can't stand by and let a lady carry her own luggage, especially after she's worked hard all day."

Tessa's jaw dropped. A lady? Papa would hoot with laughter to hear her referred to as a lady. She couldn't fault Gideon for his mistake. He was merely being polite, and in her weariness she couldn't turn down his offer. "All right. I would appreciate the help."

She led the way past the livery to the elm tree. In the gathering twilight, she glanced at Gideon, and a butterfly hiccuped in her stomach. Her nerves stood at attention. He'd already demonstrated kindness, but trust wasn't given away easily. Vulnerability invited contempt. She drew in a tentative breath. "My things are over there." She pointed toward the underbrush.

Gideon stared at her. "You mean to tell me you've been staying outside? I thought you were at Mrs. Dunnigan's."

She shrugged and continued toward the elm. "I was for one night, but I couldn't stay there indefinitely. I have no money."

"And you wouldn't take charity, is that it?"

She didn't look at him but sensed he wore the same sympathetic expression he'd worn earlier.

"You know, Tessa, there's nothing wrong with accepting help from a friend."

She wasn't sure what that word meant. She had no friends. Everything she loved was buried in the cemetery.

"Tessa?" His voice coaxed her gaze in his direction. "I thought we were friends. Friends help each other. But you can only have a friend if you be a friend."

She hardly knew what to say. He was offering something she'd never had. "Gideon, you don't know anything about me."

He walked back to the livery and picked up a lantern hanging on a post. The glow of the flame sent fingers of light dancing across his face as he returned to where she stood. "I know you loved your mother and your heart is broken. And I know you need a friend." He shifted the lantern to the other hand. "I'd like the chance to get better acquainted with you. But for now, let's get your things moved to your new place. I don't think Cully will mind if we borrow his wheelbarrow."

She was too tired to argue.

Gideon handed her the lantern and pushed the wheelbarrow from the side of the corral close to the elm. He hoisted the trunk first and balanced it over the hand grips. As he loaded the cabinet, he ran his hand over the carving on the front. "This is fine work."

"My grandfather carved that cabinet for my grandmother when they were first married. Mama brought it with her when she and Papa left Kentucky to move to Indiana. It's the only thing Mama had to remind her of her parents."

Gideon traced the intricate detail with his finger and gave a low whistle. "Your grandfather was a fine craftsman." When he turned the cabinet to steady it, the right side door wobbled. "It looks like this hinge is broken. I'd be happy to fix it for you."

Tessa shook her head. "I don't have the money."

Gideon turned with an exasperated sigh and put his hands on his hips. "There you go again. Can't you just let me fix it because I want to?"

Wariness prodded her. Nobody put themselves out without expecting something in return. She wondered if he expected favors she was unwilling to give. "Why are you being so nice to me?"

He picked up the lantern, and the light played across the space between them. His eyes studied her, but not the way the hotel clerk's did. Even in the flickering light, she saw something different about Gideon, but she couldn't distinguish what it was.

"The Bible says, *'A man that hath friends must shew himself friendly.'* I just want to be your friend, Tessa. There aren't any strings attached." He handed her the lantern and picked up the handles of the wheelbarrow. "C'mon, let's go find this place Kilgore was so generous to *give* you."

When they reached the corner of the alley bordering the hotel, Tessa halted. "If you'll please put my things right here, I can manage. Thank you for your help."

Gideon frowned. "But—"

"*Please.*"

❧

Gideon chafed at the memory of Tessa setting her jaw and insisting he leave her things at the corner. Her stubborn stance declared there was no use arguing the point. He'd done as she requested, deposited her belongings and left, but he'd fought with his pillow all night thinking about it.

The following morning as Gideon swept off the boardwalk, a friendly voice hailed him.

"Hey, Gideon."

Gideon looked up.

His friend, Ty Sawyer, set the brake on his wagon and hopped down. A thatch of blond hair stuck out in a dozen directions when he removed his sweat-stained hat, and his lopsided grin reminded Gideon of the trouble they used to get into together in their childhood days.

"Hey, Ty. Haven't seen you in town for nigh onto a month."

They tromped into the store where Ty promptly helped himself to a handful of gumdrops from the jar on the counter. "Came in for supplies. A pound of coffee, cornmeal, couple pounds of bacon, beans, some white sewing thread, and some ten-penny nails." He popped an orange gumdrop in his mouth and looked around. "Where is everybody?"

Gideon propped the broom in the corner. "Probably over at the Willow Creek Emporium."

"Hmph, Kilgore's place? It's not likely I'll ever do business with Kilgore again. That land deal soured my opinion of him."

Gideon scooped a handful of nails and dumped them into a sack. "Is this enough?"

Ty glanced into the sack. "That'll do. I had the down payment for that piece of bottomland I'd been looking at. You know the place where we used to hunt rabbits?" Without waiting for Gideon's reply, Ty continued. "Mr. Sewell said the bank would carry a loan for five years." Ty shook his head. "A week later he turned me down, and I found out it was Kilgore who denied the loan."

"How could he do that? Mr. Sewell's the bank president, not Kilgore."

Ty chewed another gumdrop. "I heard Kilgore's bought out fifty-one percent of the bank stock."

Gideon scowled. "But why would he refuse you a loan?"

Ty snorted. "Never got a straight answer on that, but you know who owns that piece of bottomland now?"

Gideon raised his eyebrows. "Not Kilgore."

"Mm-hmm."

"Why? He's not a farmer."

"No, he ain't. Mr. Sewell told me the *new owner* might sell me the property, but the price suddenly tripled."

Footsteps on the boardwalk drew Gideon's attention. Kilgore stood in the open door, an arrogant smirk on his face. He puffed his stubby cigar and ambled inside.

Ty counted out his money and handed it to Gideon before picking up his purchases. "See you around, Gideon." He headed toward the door.

"Thanks, Ty."

The young man sent a stiff nod in Kilgore's direction. "Mr. Kilgore."

Kilgore stuck his thumbs in his suspenders and replied with a condescending snort. "Sawyer." Kilgore sauntered to the counter. "Say, Maxwell, you should come to the hotel and see the pretty little tart I just hired to wait tables. She's sassy and holier than thou, but I'll tame her in short order."

The disrespectful reference to Tessa set Gideon's teeth on edge. "That's no way to talk about a lady, Kilgore."

Kilgore sneered and blew a puff of smoke in Gideon's direction. He turned and cast a wide glance around the store. "When you get ready to unload this dump, you know where to find me." He exited and strolled down the boardwalk.

Self-accusation burned in Gideon's chest. If only he could have hired Tessa himself. The prospect of Kilgore paying Tessa an honest wage for an honest day's work filled him with misgivings.

❧

Tessa's feet throbbed as she bumped open the kitchen door with her hip. Her stomach growled at the aroma of the beef stew, pork chops, steak, and fresh biscuits on her tray. She forced a smile as she placed steaming platters before three men at a corner table.

"You're new here, ain't ya?"

Tessa set a basket of warm biscuits on their table and started toward the next table where a party waited to order, but the man in the plaid shirt and leather vest grabbed her hand.

"Hey now, don't be in such a hurry." The dark-haired cowboy waggled his thick eyebrows. "Why don't you stick around, and maybe me and you can get better acquainted."

Her breath caught in her throat, and her heart accelerated as she twisted her arm trying to extract her hand.

He tightened his grip.

Her stomach constricted, and nausea rose to her throat. "Please excuse me. I have other customers."

The man's laughter drove chills down her spine, and he reeked of whiskey. "We was gonna order dessert. Maybe you can"—he cast a surreptitious glance over his shoulder and leaned toward her—"offer some suggestions."

She yanked her arm free and took a step backward. "Our dessert menu for today is"—her voice trembled—"apple pie, chocolate cake, or raisin pudding."

"Tessa!" Mr. Kilgore's voice boomed across the dining room, and every patron in the place turned in his direction.

Tessa scurried over to her boss. "Yes, sir?"

"I'm not paying you to stand around and chat. If you can't attend to your duties, I don't need you."

Tessa felt every eye in the dining room on her as she stood under the lash of Kilgore's upbraiding. Her face burned, and she couldn't gulp enough air to satisfy her lungs.

"I'm sorry, Mr. Kilgore. I tried to—"

"If your trying isn't good enough, I'll find someone else. Now get back to work, and don't let me catch you lollygagging again."

Her tongue seemed stuck to the roof of her mouth. She'd listened to Papa's tirades for as long as she could remember and survived them. Subjecting herself to Mr. Kilgore's abuse wasn't any different except that Mr. Kilgore was paying her. She needed this job.

She took orders from two other tables and scurried to the kitchen to find Flossie at the sink pumping water over her hand and groaning. "Flossie, what's wrong?"

The cook growled under her breath and continued to pump water.

Tillie spoke up as she filled the orders Tessa left on the serving counter. "She spilled hot grease over her hand. I told her to pour cold water over it."

Tessa peered over Flossie's shoulder. Angry blisters already formed on the inflamed skin. Tessa grimaced, imagining the pain.

Flossie dipped her head to one side and wailed. "What am I gonna do? If I tell Mr. Kilgore I can't work for a few days because of this, he'll fire me. This job is the only thing keepin' us goin' since our wheat crop got flooded out last year."

Tessa's heart broke for the woman. Her hands mechanically filled coffee cups and cut slices of pie as she tried to think of a way to help Flossie. Sympathy shuddered through her as she left the kitchen with her loaded tray.

As she set two plates of apple pie before a lady and a gentleman, an idea gradually formed in her head. She cleared off adjacent tables and hurried back to the kitchen where Flossie leaned forlornly against the big worktable, holding her hand in obvious agony while Tillie applied goose grease to the blisters. "Flossie, I'd like to help you."

"Why?"

Tessa blinked. Why indeed? Maybe the way Gideon helped her had something to do with it. When everyone in her world had left her, Gideon stepped forward. She remembered the verse about having friends he quoted to her. Mama taught that verse to her when she was a little girl afraid to go to school for the first time. Gideon brought it back to her memory.

She smiled at Flossie. "Because the Bible teaches if we want friends, we must first be a friend."

A furrow dented Flossie's brow. Maybe she wasn't familiar with the scripture, or she simply didn't trust Tessa. Perhaps both.

She'd have to show Flossie she was serious. "When do you usually do your baking?"

Flossie cast a doubtful look in her direction. "Early in the morning, before the breakfast crowd starts coming in. Why?"

Tessa looked at both Flossie and Tillie. "If we work

together, I think everything can still go smoothly and Flossie can keep her job." She turned to look directly at the cook. "Flossie, you can still cook. It will just take you a lot longer to do things with one hand. But we can help, can't we, Tillie?"

Tillie shrugged. "Sure. I'll help wherever I can."

Tessa gave Flossie an encouraging smile. "Tillie can lend a hand cutting up the vegetables and preparing the meat. I'll come in early, the same time you do, but I'll do the baking, and you can get started on the day's menu."

Flossie stared at Tessa while she cradled her injured hand. "You would do that for me?"

It felt good to smile. "Yes. I don't want you to lose your job, Flossie. And besides, I really enjoy baking."

Flossie grunted. "And I hate to bake. I only did it because I had to."

Tillie glanced toward the door. "What if Mr. Kilgore finds out?"

"He never comes into the kitchen, and as long as the work gets done, why should he care?"

Flossie hesitated then nodded her head. "I don't know why you're doin' this for me, but I appreciate it."

"C'mon, let's get the kitchen cleaned up and ready for tomorrow." Tessa plunged her hands into the soapy water and made short work of the dishes. In less than an hour, she slipped out the side door and made her way to the shed.

The ramshackle, lean-to structure constructed partially of sod blocks and partially of irregular widths of boards wasn't much to look at, but at least it had a roof. Unexpectedly, Gideon came to mind. She wasn't sure why it mattered to her, but she was glad he hadn't seen the place the night he helped her carry her things.

She pushed open the door. "In a few months I'll have enough saved to afford a room at Mrs. Dunnigan's place for the winter."

She pulled the much-mended quilt from the trunk and spread it on the earthen floor. Flossie had given her a leftover biscuit and a spoonful of cold gravy to take home. She added the last bit of cheese and few crackers to finish out her meager meal. As she nibbled, she pretended the biscuit was still hot and fresh and the gravy warm and savory instead of cold.

She wrapped the last two crackers in the paper to save for her breakfast, but when she started to return the bundle to the cabinet, something caught her eye. She stared hard through the shadows, trying to determine what it was. Then it moved—no, it scurried. She bit back a scream.

five

"Scat!" Tessa banged her hand on the trunk lid to scare the mouse away. She wasn't inclined to share either her quarters or her food with rodents. A shiver sent gooseflesh up her arms.

If she planned to read Mama's Bible, she'd best hurry. Night shadows loomed, driving the rays of sun behind the horizon.

Tessa took a seat in the doorway with the book angled to catch every bit of available light. She flipped pages until she came to Psalm 27. Her eyes scanned the verses she'd previously read, and she turned the page. Her lips formed the words as she read the rest of the psalm in the dusk. Her finger traced the last verse.

"Wait on the Lord: be of good courage, and he shall strengthen thine heart."

She closed the book carefully and laid it in her lap. The last bit of light faded, but the words she'd read echoed in her mind.

"It sounds like a promise. God, Mama always told me I could trust the words of this book. It says You will take me up since Mama and Papa are both gone. Does that mean You'll take care of me? Is that what I'm supposed to wait for?"

She leaned against the door frame. "And what about Gideon? He says he wants to be my friend. But what if he goes away, too?"

God's answer didn't echo from heaven.

Fatigue draped around her like a heavy cloak. She scooted aside and started to close the door only to realize she'd be closing the mice in with her.

A shudder rippled through her. Which was better—sleeping with mice or leaving the door open so anyone could enter? She shrugged at the obvious. The mice could come and go as they pleased whether she shut the door or not, and a closed door didn't offer security since there was no latch. Tomorrow she'd find a stout stick to brace the door closed.

She stretched out on one side of the quilt and pulled the other half over her. Her eyelids grew heavy as she listened for the skitter of tiny feet.

ॐ

A cacophony of laughter accosted her ears. Faces of men loomed before her, their leering eyes hungry as they reached out to grab her.

She pulled away from one only to bump against another. She gasped and whirled in the opposite direction where another man closed in. Her breath caught in her throat, strangling her screams. The men laughed as she pushed against them.

In the middle of the encroaching sea of intimidating faces was Mr. Kilgore. His stubby cigar waggled up and down as he repeated his declaration of the wages she'd earn working at the Blue Goose.

She strained for breath as panic filled her. "No, I won't! Leave me alone!"

Kilgore guffawed. "The friendlier you are, the more they buy, and if they like you, they might stick around. . .stick around. . . ."

"A man that hath friends must shew himself friendly." Gideon's smiling face came into view. "I thought we were friends. You can only have a friend if you be a friend."

She almost took a step toward him but halted abruptly when another face in the crowd pushed forward.

"You ain't worth nothin'." The hateful accusation spewed from Papa's lips. "It's your fault. You ain't worth nothin'. . . ."

Tessa lurched awake with a cry. Sweat dripped from her temples and slid down her cheek. Or was that a tear?

She consciously slowed her breathing and lay back down on the quilt. Without a clock, her only means to gauge the time was the level of noise coming from the saloon. The earlier fever pitch was now silent. She didn't know what time the establishment closed, probably the wee hours. If she allowed herself to go back to sleep, she might rise too late to help Flossie with the baking.

She rose and shook the quilt, hoping her unwelcome visitors found someplace else to spend the night. The door squeaked as she pushed it open. No illumination from the street lanterns reached the shed. Blackness enveloped the alley.

Her hands groped along the brick wall as she made her way toward the side door that opened to the hotel kitchen. Once inside, she struck a match and found the lamp hanging over the worktable. The wick caught easily, and she slid the glass globe back into place. After she fed the banked coals in the cookstove, she crossed to the cavernous pantry.

From the shelves she gathered spices, sugar, and a crock of lard. Three large baskets of apples sat beside the flour barrel.

By the time Flossie came in the side door with her hand wrapped in a clean rag, three apple pies wafted their cinnamon fragrance through the kitchen, while Tessa crimped the crust of three more on the worktable.

"Good morning, Flossie. How is your hand feeling today?"

The cook looked down at the makeshift bandage and shrugged. "Don't help to complain. I just hope it don't get no fever in it."

Tessa started to suggest Flossie have the doctor take a look at the burn but held her tongue. Doctors cost money. She bit her lip and returned to her task.

&

A week after taking over the baking, Tessa's apple pies and

chocolate cakes earned numerous compliments. Working the dough with her fingers gave her satisfaction, and pulling fragrant pastries from the oven brought a measure of contentment she'd not known for a long time.

Tillie stuck her head in the door. "Tessa, there's a girl out here who wants to know if you can make a wedding cake."

Tessa looked up from the chocolate cake she was frosting and thought for a moment. "Sure." She considered the cost of the supplies and the extra time involved. "Tell her. . .two dollars and a half."

Flossie smirked as Tillie left to deliver the message. "Don't reckon Mr. Kilgore knows about our arrangement yet, but if folks keep asking for special orders, he might wonder why."

Flossie unwrapped her hand, and Tessa crossed the kitchen to inspect the wound. The inflamed red flesh didn't appear to be healing as fast as Tessa hoped. "Flossie, you must go see the doctor."

The woman shook her head. "Even if I had the money for a doctor, I couldn't take the chance of Kilgore finding out."

Tessa wondered if Gideon carried a burn remedy at the mercantile. It couldn't hurt to ask.

The thought of Gideon ignited a warm rush of feelings— the same feelings she'd experienced when his face appeared in her awful dream a week ago. Having Gideon close by felt comfortable. Maybe because he wanted to be her friend. She refused to entertain thoughts of his being anything more.

❧

The bell on the door jingled, and Gideon looked up to see his sister, Martha, entering the mercantile. A radiant blush glowed on her cheeks, and her green eyes sparkled. "Good afternoon, big brother." She planted a kiss on Gideon's cheek.

He grinned at her. "You certainly look like there's nothing wrong in your world today."

"What could be wrong?" Martha extended her arms and

pirouetted. "God has answered my prayers, and in a few weeks, I'll be Mrs. Theodore Luskin."

Gideon smiled as peace filled his heart. Martha was marrying a fine, hardworking, Christian young man who adored her. "So what brings you to our establishment today?"

"This week's mail." She pulled the envelopes from her reticule and laid them on the counter.

She pressed her palms against the worn wood and beamed. "I just came from the hotel dining room. Their desserts are wonderful. The chocolate cake. . .mmmm." She closed her eyes and smiled as though she could taste the confection from memory.

Gideon leaned against the counter. "Did you and Ted have lunch there?"

Martha shook her head, and the gold tendrils that framed her face danced. "No, his mother came to town today so we could discuss the wedding with Pastor Witherspoon, and she took me to the hotel for lunch. We asked if the cook could make a wedding cake, and she said yes."

Gideon frowned. He didn't wish to deny his sister, but even the smallest luxuries cost money. "Did you happen to get a price for this cake?"

Martha's countenance fell, and her voice lost some of its joy. "She said two dollars and a half."

Gideon felt like a cad. His declining business wasn't Martha's worry. How could he rob her of her happy anticipation? He reached over and patted her hand. "Go ahead and order the cake, honey." *I'll manage to pay for it somehow.*

His sister came around the counter and hugged him. "Oh, thank you, Gideon. I'll see you tonight at supper."

He bid her good-bye and watched her dash up the stairs to their living quarters. He wished his parents could have lived long enough to see their daughter married. How pleased Pa would have been to walk Martha down the aisle.

Troubling thoughts of Tessa arose once again. The way her father hurled horrible accusations at her sickened him. Gideon puzzled over Langford's unreasonable attack on Tessa. How could the man possibly blame her for her mother's death? He couldn't imagine his own father telling Martha she was worthless. On the contrary, his father adored his daughter. He shook his head and breathed a prayer for Tessa's safety and comfort. Her welfare had become a regular request whenever he communed with God.

He sorted through the mail. The return address on one envelope made his heart leap—the long-awaited answer from a horse breeder in Illinois. He tore open the flap and extracted the missive. A smile climbed into his face as he read. The man was willing to sell him a Belgian stallion at a reasonable price. The letter included terms and suggestions for taking delivery.

The only thing standing between him and his dream of owning a spread and breeding horses was the sale of the mercantile. Now with the promise of a stallion, he allowed himself to daydream about a pasture full of fine animals, bred especially for the needs of farmers—powerful horses that could pull a plow or a heavy wagon and help a farmer clear a field of rocks and stumps, yet gentle enough to take the family to church on Sunday. If he accepted Kilgore's offer, he could move ahead with his plans. Despite the foul taste left in his mouth whenever he thought about the man, Kilgore's offer looked better all the time.

The door's jingling bell interrupted his thoughts as Pearl Dunnigan walked in. "Good afternoon, Gideon."

He tucked the letter away. "Hello, Miss Pearl. What can I do for you today?"

The smiling woman reached into her reticule. "It's pretty much the same list every week. Whenever I try to change the menu, my boarders complain that they'd rather have the same fried chicken and pot roast."

Gideon grinned. Miss Pearl's fried chicken was legendary, and her pot roast was fork tender and juicy. "I don't blame them."

She shook her head. "It gets tiring sometimes, especially since I'm getting older. Standing in the kitchen for hours isn't as easy as it was ten years ago. I thought I'd try to get some fresh fruit for dessert instead of having to prepare something."

Gideon glanced at her as he weighed the amount of sugar she needed. "I hear tell the hotel dining room is turning out some pretty good pies and cakes. Martha's planning to order her wedding cake from there. Maybe you could give yourself a break and pick up a couple of pies."

Miss Pearl put her hands on her hips. "Why, Gideon Maxwell, what an excellent idea. You know Mr. Clemmons who boards at my place thinks Mr. Kilgore must have hired himself a new cook."

Her observation gave Gideon pause. Kilgore said Tessa was waiting tables. "That a fact?"

Mrs. Dunnigan laughed. "You know what a gossip Mr. Clemmons is, so anything he says is purely speculation."

Gideon scooped dried beans into a bag to weigh them. "I might go over there myself and sample some pie. Maybe I'll take Martha along so she can see what an apple pie is supposed to taste like."

"Oh, Gideon, shame on you. You shouldn't pick on Martha so. She'll be a fine cook someday."

Gideon didn't put much effort in his attempt to appear repentant. "If I didn't pick on her, she'd think I didn't love her."

"Tsk-tsk. Gideon Maxwell, you're terrible." Miss Pearl shook her head.

Gideon winked at her. "Did you want any molasses or

bacon to go with these beans?"

"Hmm, five pounds of bacon, and go ahead and throw in a tin of molasses. Maybe I'll bake some cookies next week."

Gideon accommodated her request and tucked in a couple of the dear lady's favorite peppermint sticks.

Miss Pearl counted out her money, and he carried the loaded box out to the little cart she always pulled along behind her when she ran her errands. "Thank you, Gideon. Now don't you be a stranger. You come and see my Maggie's new batch of kittens."

Gideon grinned. "Haven't you told Maggie she's too old for such nonsense? How many years have you had that old cat?"

"Oh, nigh onto fifteen years, I think. Anyway, this is the cutest litter she's ever had. Maybe Martha would like to pick one out. She's going to be living out on the Luskins' farm. They'll need a good mouser."

"Yes, ma'am, I'll ask her. You have a nice afternoon now." He paused in the doorway and considered Miss Pearl's comment about Kilgore hiring a new cook. Could it be Tessa was doing more than just waiting tables?

He glanced up and down the boardwalk. No throngs of customers demanded his attention. It wouldn't hurt to run over to the hotel for a piece of pie.

He locked the door and hurried down the boardwalk. His long strides covered the distance to the hotel in no time. Most of the lunch patrons had already departed when he entered the archway that led to the dining room. He sat down hoping for a glimpse of Tessa.

Instead the regular waitress came over to his table to take his order.

"Hello, Tillie. Do you have any apple pie left?"

Tillie smiled. "It's been going fast these days, but we're turning them out as fast as we sell them. Is that all you want, just pie?"

"And coffee. Thanks."

Tillie hurried away and returned moments later with a generous slab of apple pie and a steaming cup of coffee. "Fifteen cents."

Gideon pulled out two dimes and told Tillie to keep the change. The spicy aroma teased his senses, and his mouth began to water before he tasted the first bite. When the still-warm apples and cinnamon wrapped in flaky crust hit his tongue, he closed his eyes and savored the sweetness. It was beyond any doubt the best apple pie in the county. Would it be too bold for him to ask who made it?

Tillie returned a minute later. "More coffee?"

"No, thanks. But I would like to compliment your cook on this wonderful pie." He waited with hopeful anticipation to learn the identity of the baker.

Confusion traced lines across Tillie's forehead, and she cast a glance over her shoulder. "We all pitch in and share the kitchen duties."

Disappointment pricked him. He'd hoped Tessa was the one turning out the delectable desserts. "Did you make this pie? It's certainly the best I ever ate."

"N–no, it wasn't me." After another nervous glance from side to side, she leaned down to whisper to Gideon. "Actually, we have a new girl who was hired to wait tables, but she's been doing the baking since our cook burned her hand."

So it *was* Tessa! But why did Tillie seem to think Tessa's baking skills should be kept secret?

"If Mr. Kilgore finds out Flossie hurt her hand and isn't doing everything she's supposed to do, he'll fire her. Tessa, the girl who's doing the baking, came up with a plan for her and me to help out so Flossie won't lose her job. In fact, we were wondering if you have anything at the mercantile to use on burns."

Gideon's heart smiled at the thought of Tessa stepping up

to help the injured cook, but outwardly he frowned. "Hasn't she seen the doctor?"

Tillie shook her head vehemently.

He pressed his lips together and thought for a moment. "Let me see what I can do."

The waitress smiled in obvious relief. "Thank you."

Gideon shoveled the rest of pie into his mouth and pressed his fork on the remaining crumbs, unwilling to waste a single morsel. He drained his coffee and rose to leave.

On his way out, his eye caught a glimpse of motion from the second-floor balcony. When his gaze darted upward, he discovered Kilgore standing at the railing, watching him walk across the lobby.

six

Gideon itched to contact the man in Illinois regarding the purchase of the stallion, but first things first. A piece of acreage he'd looked at awhile back, land perfectly suited for his dream, called to him. As far as he knew, the parcel remained available.

When he and Martha returned home from church and finished eating Sunday dinner, he walked over to the livery. "Howdy, Cully!"

The old curmudgeon snorted as he startled awake. "Gideon! Why you sneakin' up on a body like that? It's plumb dangerous to come up behind a man, y'know."

Gideon grinned at the gray-haired old coot. "You don't look too dangerous to me, sleeping in that haystack, Cully. Now some of those swayback, lop-eared nags in the corral are another matter. How much do you charge to rent one of those prized steeds?"

Cully brushed off his overalls and picked hay from his scraggly beard. He waved a gnarled hand in the direction of the corral. "Take your pick. If you saddle him yourself, I won't charge you nothin'."

"Thanks, Cully."

Gideon snagged the halter of the nearest horse. Minutes later he tightened the cinch and mounted. Reining the animal through the corral gate, he set off toward the east at a lope.

It'd been months since he'd looked over this piece of land. As he rode, he pictured in his mind every draw and grassy slope and the small creek that meandered through the prime grazing pasture.

He scanned the landscape and found the outcropping of

boulders that served as the landmark. He reined the gelding in the direction of what he hoped would someday become his spread. A grove of aspens quivered in the breeze along the northern boundary of the parcel, and the slope was dotted with cottonwoods and birches.

He walked the horse along a line where he imagined sturdy fences for a corral and a large barn for housing his brood mares. Beyond that, the perfect spot for a house came into view, up on a rise surrounded by scrub junipers and sheltered by a stand of white pines and cedars. The creek sang as the water tumbled down the slope and leveled out into the grazing land. If he could have painted a picture of his dream, this would be it.

First thing Monday morning, he planned to be at the land office to confirm the availability of the land. If his dream was to be reality, however, the sale of the mercantile still hung over his head. Kilgore's smug smile tainted his ambition.

He lingered awhile longer, turning his plans over in his head. No need to hurry back since it was Sunday. He dismounted and looped the reins around a low-hanging branch. After taking a moment to inhale the fragrance of the thick spring grass, he hiked up to the spot where he thought to build the house.

The area was elevated just high enough to overlook the acreage spreading out before him. He needed nothing grand in a house but hoped one day to bring a wife to this place and raise a family. There was plenty of room on the rise for a good-sized house, a kitchen garden, a chicken coop, and a grassy area for children to play. In his mind's eye, he saw smoke coming from a stone chimney and a woman hanging laundry on the clothesline with a toddler clinging to her apron. Unexpectedly Tessa's face eased into his thoughts.

Startled, he blinked and the image melted from his mind. When he stopped to consider the idea, he realized Tessa's tender heart and uncomplaining spirit had already endeared her to him. She possessed a spirit of determination that made him smile.

He paused and invited his mind to once again entertain the possibility. Was it so unreasonable to ponder? True, he didn't know a great deal about her other than the love and respect she'd had for her mother and that her father abused then abandoned her. But the very fact that she wasted no time seeking employment and resisted help bespoke of her character. She was unspoiled, wanted a handout from no one, and didn't hesitate to befriend the hotel cook when the woman had a need.

He strolled across the imaginary front porch and leaned down to pluck a few daisies growing where he thought the fireplace ought to be built. He envisioned a warm, comfortable room with a rocking chair beside the hearth. Once more Tessa appeared in the picture, taking her ease in the rocker with a small babe in her arms.

"This is ridiculous. I hardly know the girl." He was glad there was no one about to read his foolish reflections.

But why were they foolish? He and Tessa were friends. What was to stop him from getting to know her better? The idea was not at all unpleasant.

A winsome thought wandered through his mind. "I wonder if Tessa likes daisies." His mouth tweaked with a smile. "Only one way to find out." He bent to add a dozen more flowers to his few and then pulled some long prairie grasses to tie the bunch together.

As he strode back to where the horse was tethered and munching the sweet meadow grass, Gideon's step hesitated. Did Tessa work on Sunday? How should he approach her to hand her the flowers? Knock on the kitchen door? The horse turned his head and gave Gideon a woeful look. "How should I know if she's working today?"

The horse gave an answering snort and shook his head as he pawed the ground. The only thing that interested the beast was heading back to the barn.

"Come on, horse. Let's go." He tucked the stems of the daisies inside his shirt and swung into the saddle. All the way back to town he accused himself of getting off track. After all, the purpose of his excursion was to take another look at the parcel of land he wanted to purchase, not daydream about the woman with whom he might one day share that land.

Gideon shook off the guilt. It wasn't unimaginable to want a wife and family one day as long as he didn't allow his priorities to become out of order. Wanting the kind of marriage his parents had was a fine aspiration. But his first priority was selling the mercantile and purchasing the land. Next, he'd strike a deal with the man from Illinois to purchase a stallion. Finding a wife should come later, after he had a place to offer her.

When he arrived back in Willow Creek, the first person he spotted was Henry Kilgore. Why did it always seem like the man was watching him? Kilgore thrust out his chest and hooked his thumbs in his suspenders, the ever-present cigar hanging out one side of his mouth. As Gideon rode past on his way to the livery, Kilgore nodded to him with a half smirk, like he knew to whom Gideon planned to give the daisies.

Walking into the dining room and handing Tessa the flowers was a stupid plan anyway. The last thing he wanted to do was embarrass her or jeopardize her job. If he couldn't think of a better idea, he'd wind up taking the flowers home to Martha.

&

"I'm telling you, I think you should open a bakery. Just look at these orders. Three whole cakes and five whole pies, and that doesn't include all the servings we sell to the diners every day."

Tessa brushed a floury hand across her chin and continued rolling out piecrusts. Tillie's imagination was running away with her. "Where would I get the money to start a bakery? Sure, I like the idea, and I truly do enjoy baking, but just think of everything I would need."

Flossie snorted. "It ain't likely you'll ever make enough money here, working for Kilgore."

It was true. Her wages barely covered her thrifty needs. The old sock she used to tuck away a bit of savings toward her winter rent remained pitifully slack. How she wished she could afford to look elsewhere for a better paying job. When she made up her mind to survive, she took the first job that came along. Now she feared finding anything better was a fairy tale.

Tillie shrugged. "It's nice to dream."

Tessa had to admit it was an admirable goal, albeit an impossible one. She lifted her shoulders. "I appreciate your compliment. It was a very nice thing to say."

Flossie turned her head to look at Tessa. "We've got a problem, you know."

"What problem?"

Flossie held up her hand. "My hand is getting better since I started using that Porter's Liniment Salve Gideon Maxwell gave me. I can't keep expecting you to do all the baking. But the customers didn't rave about my desserts like they do yours, and if I start doing the baking again, we'll start losing business."

Tessa barely heard Flossie's description of what she deemed a problem. Her focus hung on the cook's first statement. "Gideon gave you that salve? I thought you'd gone to the doctor."

Flossie shook her head, and another lock of mousy brown

hair escaped its pins. "No, Gideon brought it from the mercantile. I tried to tell him I didn't have money to pay him, but he just said I needed the salve now and I could pay him later. He told me to soak my hand in eucalyptus tea, too." She turned her hand over to show the healing blisters to Tessa. "See how much better it looks?"

Tessa arched her eyebrows. "That was a very kind thing for him to do." But Gideon's kindness wasn't a surprise. She'd already been the beneficiary of his thoughtfulness more than once. Perhaps it was true that not all men were like Papa. They weren't all drunkards, nor did they all care only for themselves.

"What do you think?"

Tessa's face warmed. What did she think? She thought Gideon Maxwell was a very nice man. Very nice indeed. "About what?"

"Weren't you paying attention? I asked you what you think we should do now that my hand is getting better. Fact is, I should be able to start doing the baking again in another day or two."

Tessa folded the pastry dough over and laid it into the pie plate in front of her. "I haven't given it much thought. I rather like doing the baking. Tillie does more of the serving than I do, although I help her as much as I can. You really do have your hands full just cooking the meals."

Flossie put her hands on her ample hips and stared at her. "Tessa, you're only getting paid thirty-five cents a day because Mr. Kilgore still doesn't know you're doing all the baking."

Tessa shrugged. "The tips have gotten a lot better."

Flossie laughed. "That's because folks love your desserts, not to mention your biscuits, your white bread, and your yeast rolls. The tips won't be as good when they start eating the stuff I bake again."

Tessa and Tillie exchanged looks. "Flossie, you aren't thinking about telling Mr. Kilgore, are you?"

Worry lines dug trenches across Flossie's forehead, and she turned back to the stove. "I don't want to. But it's not right that you're doin' so much work and not gettin' paid for it, Tessa. Before you came here, I'd never had anyone do something so nice for me like you did."

Tessa heard a sniff coming from Flossie's direction. She didn't know what to say. The feeling Flossie described was familiar to her. The day they buried Mama, she experienced more kindness than she'd ever thought existed in the world, and she didn't know what to do to repay the people like the preacher, Mrs. Dunnigan, and Gideon. Especially Gideon.

"Why don't we just continue the way we are? I'm not complaining. I keep trying to tell you I like to bake. It's more enjoyable than waiting tables and dodging rude men." She slid three pies into the oven and wiped her hands on a towel. "As soon as those pies come out of the oven, these loaves of bread will be ready to go in. I'm going to go help Tillie clear tables."

Several diners lingered at their tables over second cups of coffee.

Tessa removed plates and bowls and collected as many compliments as she did tips. She smiled and thanked the patrons and encouraged them to come again. With her tray loaded, she balanced it carefully through the kitchen doors and traded it for a clean, empty one. "Flossie, can you check the water reservoir to make sure we have plenty of hot water? I'll be right back and start these dishes."

Tray in hand, she pushed the kitchen door open again and headed for the other side of the dining room. At the second table, she came face-to-face with Gideon Maxwell.

"Hello there."

"Hello, Gideon. It's nice to see you. Did you enjoy your meal?"

Gideon smiled. "I ate dinner at home. My sister, Martha, is trying to learn to cook before she gets married in a couple of months, and I'm her victim. That is, I'm her loving big brother, so I have to—I mean, I *get* to—eat everything she cooks."

His smile as well as his teasing comment about his sister warmed her and made her wonder what it might be like to sit across the table from him and listen to his rich voice and watch his eyes twinkle. She'd wanted to know him better from the first day she met him, but it hardly seemed appropriate, his being a business owner and her nothing more than a serving girl.

"Do you need more coffee?"

"No, thanks. I just stopped in for a slice of the best apple pie this side of the Mississippi River, and I don't want to wash the taste out of my mouth with coffee."

Heat filled her face, and she couldn't keep from smiling. She lowered her eyes and reached to take his empty plate, noting there wasn't a single crumb left on it.

"I understand you are the one doing the baking."

She caught her breath and glanced to the right and left. "We'd rather nobody knew about that."

Gideon gave her a knowing look. "You mean you'd rather Kilgore didn't know about it."

She didn't know how he'd become privy to the information, but she merely nodded. Gideon could be trusted. "I really like doing it. Tillie even told me I should open a bakery. Of course that's ridiculous. Opening a new business takes money, and I don't make that much. But it was fun to think about."

Gideon nodded. "That does sound like an interesting idea. You should give it some consideration. Maybe you could get a loan from the bank."

"Pfft! Me? Why would the bank want to loan me money? No, it's silly to even allow myself to dream about such a thing."

Gideon appeared to be about to disagree when his expression darkened abruptly.

A hand grabbed Tessa's upper arm and jerked her around. Mr. Kilgore's ferocious expression bore down on her like an awakening grizzly in springtime. "Didn't I tell you not to stand around dawdling?" His fingers dug into her flesh so hard she winced.

Gideon was on his feet in an instant, grabbing hold of Mr. Kilgore's arm. "Let go of her, Kilgore!"

Her boss pulled away from Gideon so forcefully she nearly dropped her tray and lost her footing. "Gideon, please. It's all right. I shouldn't have stopped to talk. I'm sorry, Mr. Kilgore. It won't happen again."

Gideon grabbed the man's jacket lapel and necktie all in one powerful grip. "I said let go of her, Kilgore."

"Who do you think you are, ordering me around in my own hotel? I have half a mind to call the sheriff and have you thrown out of here."

The man's bluster didn't make Gideon back down an inch. As soon as Mr. Kilgore released Tessa's arm, Gideon turned loose of the man's garments.

Mr. Kilgore swore and pointed to the door. "Get out, and don't you set foot in here again."

Tessa's heart pounded in her ears. Fear dug cruel claws up her throat, as she held her breath, anticipating the men coming to blows.

Mr. Kilgore whirled around to growl in her face. "You're fired. Clear out of here." He tossed a few coins at her feet. "That should cover whatever I owe you."

The flinch that shuddered through her felt too familiar.

seven

Tessa stooped and picked up the coins with a trembling hand. When Papa left her, she thought groveling at a man's feet would become nothing more than an ugly memory, but she was wrong. She could feel Mr. Kilgore's glare boring into her, but the man wouldn't have the pleasure of seeing her cry.

Ignoring the stares of the diners, she fixed her eyes on the kitchen door and walked resolutely between the tables. No more exchanges between Gideon and Mr. Kilgore roared behind her, so she assumed Gideon had left as well.

As soon as the kitchen door closed behind her, she sagged against the worktable and let the tears come.

Flossie and Tillie came immediately to her side.

Flossie patted her on the back. "We heard him bellowing all the way in here."

Tillie slipped an awkward arm around Tessa's shoulders. "I'm so sorry, Tessa."

Tessa dried her eyes with the corner of her apron. "Those pies ought to be just about ready to come out, and the bread is ready to go in."

"Oh, who cares? Let the old buzzard bake his own pies."

Tessa shot a glance at Tillie. "Don't let them burn, or Flossie might get fired, too. Remember, he thinks she's doing the baking." She hung up her apron and exited the side door, only to run squarely into Gideon.

Remorse defined the lines carved in his forehead. "Tessa, I'm so sorry you got fired. But I couldn't sit there and let him put his hands on you."

She stared at him in astonishment.

He must have taken her silence for anger, because contrition filled his tone. "I apologize. It doesn't change anything, and it's my fault you got fired. Please allow me to help you find another job."

Words failed her. Never in all of her nineteen years had she ever seen a man apologize for anything, much less for losing his temper. Twice now Gideon had sprung to her defense. Her eyes remained riveted on his face, and the words she wanted to speak refused to line up in the right order.

"I. . .It. . .it wasn't. . .your fault. I. . .I—"

Gideon grasped both her hands. "Did he hurt you? Is your arm all right?"

Lucidity finally made its way back to her brain. "Yes."

"Yes, he hurt you?"

"No, he didn't hurt me, and yes, my arm is all right. Gideon, why?" Her hands seemed to not have a purpose. She clasped them together and held them to her chin. "*Why* did you get angry? Why did you grab him? I'm not worth your trouble."

Gideon jerked his head up, his eyes darkened. "Don't say that, Tessa. You shouldn't believe those things your father told you. You're a lady, and I will never stand idly by while a lady is treated disrespectfully." The anger on his face softened. "And besides that, you're not just any lady. You're. . . well, you're special."

His face flushed crimson. Perhaps he didn't mean to say what he'd just said. Maybe, like her, he had a hard time putting words together when he was upset. At any rate, his hangdog look spoke volumes. He regretted what happened— but did he regret defending her, or was he just sorry she'd lost her job?

"Well, thank you, Gideon. Don't worry. Something will work out. Mama always said tomorrow will be brighter."

He gave her a tiny smile, lifted his fingers in a half wave, and walked away.

She turned and walked toward the shed. Maybe Mr. Kilgore wouldn't care if she stayed there tonight. She hadn't planned on having to look for a new place to live so soon.

She turned the corner at the end of the alley and stopped short. Stuck in the door handle of the shed was a bouquet of daisies. They looked rather forlorn and slightly wilted, but they seemed to echo Gideon's words. She was worth something, even if it was just a bunch of wildflowers.

If they were from Gideon, it meant he knew where she was living, but somehow it didn't seem to matter. She reversed her direction and trotted down the alley to see which way Gideon had gone.

Just as she reached the boardwalk, Mr. Kilgore stepped out the front door of the hotel. "Ah, there you are."

What did he want? Whatever it was, it couldn't be anything good.

"I suppose you've learned your lesson. In fact, I wondered if you had given any more thought to my previous offer. If you can't manage to serve tables efficiently in the dining room, maybe you're better suited to a different type of establishment. You know, standing around and flirting with my clients at the Blue Goose might make you one of the favorites over there. They like it when the girls are nice to them. What do you say?"

Her mouth dropped open at his audacity, and she snapped it shut before she said something she'd regret. Did he expect her to lick his boots for telling her she could work serving whiskey? Besides, according to Tillie and Flossie, the girls who worked at the saloon did more than just serve drinks. Tessa didn't want to think about what other duties they might have to perform. Maybe the kind of work Mr. Kilgore suggested was the best she could be, but the unceasing tug on her heart reminded her that Gideon thought her to be a lady. She took a deep breath and met Mr. Kilgore's icy eyes. "No, Mr. Kilgore. I will not work in your saloon. Good day."

She started to go around him, but he stretched out his hand to stop her. Her feet froze, and she glared at his hand touching her arm, then up at his face, and back down at his hand.

Mr. Kilgore lifted his hand from her arm and held it slightly aloft, scorn coloring the sneer on his face. With methodic motion, he splayed his fingers and slid his thumbs down his suspenders and cleared his throat. "I understand you're the one who's been doing the baking."

Her pulse skipped a beat. They'd been so careful to keep their secret. She feared for Flossie's job, but she lifted her chin and tried her best to appear poised. "That's right. Flossie burned her hand, and she was afraid you'd fire her. I didn't want to see her lose her job, so I helped out." She again started around him.

This time he had the good sense to keep his hands to himself. "Miss Langford, I've changed my mind. I'm feeling rather generous today, so you can have your job back."

Tessa cocked one eyebrow at him. "At thirty-five cents a day?"

"Well, since you're doing the baking, I could raise you to forty-five cents."

She turned to face him squarely. "Fifty cents and Flossie gets to keep her job."

Mr. Kilgore's face reddened. Though a vein popped out on his neck and his lips tightened around his cigar, she didn't blink.

"All right! Fifty cents." He yanked the stubby cigar from his mouth and pointed it at her. "But you remember one thing. Nobody tells me what to do. Not you or that hypocrite Gideon Maxwell. I don't take that sanctimonious rot from anybody, and don't you forget it. You watch your step." He huffed and stalked down the boardwalk.

An odd mixture of laughter, tears, relief, and disgust welled inside her. Her pulse drummed in her temples, and she couldn't decide whether to look for Gideon or return to her humble dwelling. Instead she did neither. Her knees began to shake, and she sat down on the boardwalk, her lungs heaving like she'd just run a race.

⁊⦿

Gideon slammed the door of the living quarters above the mercantile. Fortunately Martha wasn't home to witness his tantrum. Anger seethed through him at the thought of Kilgore manhandling Tessa. His feet refused to stay still, so he paced back and forth across the front room. He wished he could have thrown at least one punch—just one—square in the mouth.

"He's insufferable!"

"Henry Kilgore may not have behaved like a gentleman, but you're not behaving like one either. Kilgore has an excuse. He's not a Christian. You are."

Gideon flopped down on the settee and sighed. "I know, Lord. Now Tessa's lost her job, and it's my fault."

He slid to the floor and knelt, leaning his elbows on the settee and holding his face in his hands. "Father, please help Tessa find another job. I hated that she was working for Kilgore, but now she has nothing. She probably won't accept any help from me. Whatever the solution, it will have to come from You." He remained on his knees for a time, asking God to forgive his display of temper and praying for Tessa's situation.

After a while, he felt the urge to go downstairs and work off some of his aggravation.

He'd been meaning to rearrange things in the storeroom for a long time. If the place was better organized with increased shelf space, the mercantile might be more attractive to a buyer.

He rummaged around, pushing and shoving crates here and there, and sketching some shelving ideas on a tablet. A large lumpy object hid under an old canvas in the corner, and Gideon groaned when he remembered the cookstove his father had ordered three years ago for a customer who never came back to get it. The thing took up so much space out front that Gideon finally dragged it back to the storeroom and covered it, thinking he could at least stack bales of fence wire on it.

He pulled off the canvas and scowled at the behemoth. Maybe if he put a reduced price on it and hauled it back out front, someone might take it off his hands. He gripped the thing and pushed and pulled, grunting until sweat popped out on his forehead and dribbled down his face.

Finally, after twenty minutes of wrestling, he straightened up and glared at the stove. The monstrosity simply didn't want to move.

Whatever the solution, it will have to come from You.

An idea began taking shape in his mind. He grabbed the tablet that bore his rough sketches and crumpled the page. With pencil in hand, a new plan unfolded on a fresh sheet of paper. He sketched efficient shelving and storage, a work space, and a new display area.

An hour later, the plan lay before him on the tablet. "Lord, if this is what You want me to do, You'll have to make all the details work. But don't let me run ahead of You, Father. This has to be Your plan, not mine."

Gideon slapped his hat on his head and bounded out the back door with the tablet in hand. The next step was to speak to Pearl Dunnigan. He took the stairs leading to her back porch two at a time and rapped on her door.

She opened the door and smiled broadly. "Why, Gideon! How nice of you to drop by. Please come in."

He swept off his hat. "Afternoon, Miss Pearl. Would you have a few minutes to talk?"

"Of course. Come sit down at the kitchen table." She bustled about pouring two cups of coffee.

The aroma of Sunday pot roast lingered in the spacious kitchen. He wiped his feet on the braided rug at the door. Cheery red-checkered curtains framed the wide window from which sunlight flooded the room. Clay flowerpots lined up like fence posts along the windowsill.

Miss Pearl ushered him to a bare, work-worn table in the middle of the room. Gideon sat on a creaking chair and laid his tablet in front of him, while Miss Pearl set out a plate heaped with molasses cookies and joined him at the table.

He took a tentative sip of the steaming coffee. "I have something I'd like to discuss with you." He pushed the tablet over so she could look at his sketches.

Thirty minutes later, Miss Pearl shared Gideon's excitement. She clapped her hands. "Oh, Gideon, I can't tell you how I'm looking forward to this."

Gideon emptied his coffee mug. "Tessa can be in business for herself, and she can have a decent place to live here while she helps you out with the baking. Plus, the baked goods she'll sell from the mercantile will be her source of income while it brings more customers into the store."

"I have a little room behind the kitchen stairs that will be perfect for her." Miss Pearl blotted her lips with the hem of her apron. "I've been using it for storage, so it will take me a few days to get it ready."

Gideon rose and picked up the tablet. "There's no rush since it will take me at least a couple of weeks to construct the work area and install the stove." Even as he spoke the words, he wished he could make it happen today.

"When will you tell her?"

He paused by the door. "I'd like to get the storeroom

organized into a work space first. That way, I'll have something to show her." Guilt still hounded him over the events of the afternoon. "I just hope she doesn't think of it as charity."

❧

Tessa darted out the door and made straight for Maxwell's Mercantile. Telling Gideon she still had a job wasn't the only reason for her errand. When she'd opened up the cabinet this morning to retrieve the leftover cinnamon bread she'd brought home, she discovered little ragged holes chewed through the paper, and only a few miniscule crumbles of bread remained. The little beasts had also made a feast of the crackers she'd bought just two days before.

The mercantile door stood open, inviting her inside.

"Hello, Gideon."

When he looked up, his normal polite smile he used to greet all his customers deepened into something she didn't dare try to interpret. "Hi, Tessa."

Her heart skipped. "I wanted you to know that Mr. Kilgore gave me my job back."

"Oh?"

The scowl on his face surprised her. She thought he'd be happy she still had a job. "After you left yesterday, Mr. Kilgore came looking for me. He said he knew I'd been doing the baking and he'd changed his mind about firing me."

Gideon shrugged. "Hmph. More likely he was afraid he'd lose business without you doing the baking."

"I don't know about that, but he gave me a raise."

"That a fact? But Tessa, if he ever dares to lay a hand—"

She stopped him. "Don't worry. I don't think he will." She tilted her head to one side. "By any chance do you know who left a lovely bouquet of daisies at my door yesterday?"

If the red stain filling Gideon's cheeks was evidence, she had her answer. "Thank you. They're lovely. You keep doing things that puzzle me. I can't understand why you want to be nice to someone like me."

Gideon bristled and put his hands on his hips. "Now don't start that again." He held his hands out, palms up, in an entreaty. "Tessa, I just can't understand why your father railed at you so, and I certainly can't understand why you believe the things he said to you."

She lifted her shoulders in a resigned shrug. "It seemed like I heard him say things like that all my life. I was. . .well, a disappointment to him." She dipped her head. "Mama had a very difficult time—" Heat filled her face. "After I was born, she never regained her strength. I don't ever remember Mama being healthy." Her voice became raspy. "She was never able to give Papa the son he wanted, and it was because of me." The memory of Mama's soft whisper in the night after Papa's tirades, telling Tessa how much she loved her, stroked her heart. But Mama feared Papa, too.

Gideon shook his head. "Tessa, he was wrong. You are a lady, and you don't deserve to be treated otherwise. Please believe that."

She lifted her shoulders. "I don't know. It may take some time."

"We'll work on it." His grin nearly knocked her breath from her. "Was there anything you needed?"

"Well, yes. I need to know the price of a crock or a canister, something with a lid tight enough to keep out a mouse."

His expression turned sympathetic, and he pulled two sizes of crockery off a high shelf and set them before her on the counter. "This larger one is twenty-eight cents, and the smaller is eighteen cents. Which size would suit your needs?"

Her hand felt around in her pocket for the coins Mr. Kilgore tossed at her yesterday. She hesitated. The smaller one would do nicely, but she wanted to put the coins in her pocket into the old sock she was using to stash away her savings toward her winter rent. Now that Mr. Kilgore had given her a raise, perhaps she could part with eighteen cents later in the week.

She ran a finger around the edge of the smaller crock. "I think I'll wait for now."

"Look, Tessa." He pushed the crock toward her. "Why don't you take this with you now. You can pay me later."

She stiffened and shook her head slightly, nudging the crock back across the counter to him. No, she'd not take anything without being able to pay cash for it. "When I get my pay this week, I'll come back and get it. Meanwhile, could I get five cents' worth of cheese and crackers, please?" She fished a nickel from her pocket.

He sighed. "Sure." He went behind the counter and sliced a generous wedge from the large round of cheese.

"That's too much, Gideon. I said five cents' worth."

He put one hand on his hip in mock indignation. "Are you trying to tell me how to run my store?" He wrapped the cheese in paper and went over to a wooden barrel to scoop out a large handful of crackers. "Tessa, is this all you're eating? Cheese and crackers?"

"No. Flossie said I can take some of the leftovers home at the end of the day." She pushed the nickel across the counter and picked up the paper-wrapped bundle. "But Flossie has a family to feed, so I usually make sure she takes home most of the leftovers."

She thanked him and started for the door.

"Tessa?"

She turned.

"God says you are precious in His sight, and I agree with Him."

eight

Gideon watched as the bank president glanced over the statement from the land office. When Gideon learned the land was owned by the bank, he'd stopped by to speak with Roland Sewell to inquire about the price and terms.

The portly man behind the desk cleared his throat. "This is a fine piece of land. The man who intended to farm it had a run of bad luck and defaulted on his loan." Sewell stroked his gray whiskers. "The board of directors meets Wednesday. I will bring your request before them at that time."

Gideon picked up the document and folded it. "The final agreement will have to wait until I have a buyer for the mercantile."

Mr. Sewell stood and offered his hand. "That's fine. There's no rush."

Gideon shook the man's hand and exited the bank.

Down the street, the stage pulled up to the depot amid swirling dust. The door opened, and a man wearing a tweed suit with a fancy vest and bowler hat disembarked. Gideon didn't recall seeing the man before. He'd surely remember a dandy dressed like that.

Gideon simply shrugged. None of his concern. He unlocked the mercantile doors and turned the sign over that declared the store open.

He set to work measuring and marking the walls for the new shelving in the storeroom. His carpentry skills wouldn't win any prizes, but he'd learned enough from his father to know which end of a hammer to use.

"Hello, anyone about?"

Gideon hurried from the storeroom to greet his customer. To his surprise, it was the fancy gentleman he'd seen earlier getting off the stage. The man's neatly trimmed mustache and side muttonchops were sprinkled with silver. "Good morning, sir. Welcome to Willow Creek."

The man smiled broadly. "Ah, you Westerners. Such a friendly lot, you are. My name is Behr, Hubert Behr." Mr. Behr's curious accent sounded European. "You're pretty well stocked here, I see. I need several articles—shaving soap, some pipe tobacco, writing paper, and a pot of ink. Linen handkerchiefs, if you have them. Also, I need some footwear more suitable to this area."

"Of course. Right this way, sir."

When Mr. Behr made his choices, Gideon tallied up the man's purchases. "Shall I deliver these for you, or would you like to take them with you?"

"You deliver, do you? Well, then just deliver them to the hotel down the street. I'll pick them up at the front desk after I've finished my business." He handed Gideon an extra silver dollar. "Take this for your trouble, young man."

When Gideon started to protest, Mr. Behr waved his hand. "I insist. You're saving me an extra trip." He touched the brim of his bowler in farewell as he exited.

He was a pleasant enough fellow. A smile tweaked Gideon's lips at the man's attire. His fancy suit, vest, and hat were as out of place in Willow Creek as a cattle rustler at a tea party. He slipped the silver dollar into his pocket with a grin. *That'll help pay for Martha's wedding cake.*

For the next two hours he worked feverishly on the shelves. When he finished, he stepped back and admired his work. The simple pine planks were plain, but they were serviceable, sturdy, and within easy reach for Tessa.

The bell on the front door sounded.

Gideon laid his hammer down and exited the storeroom to

serve his customer but halted in the doorway. "What are you doing here, Kilgore?"

Kilgore smirked and looked around. "It appears your customers are staying away in droves. Your creditors will be knocking on your door before long with their hands out. I'd like to be around then, when you regret not taking my first offer to buy this place."

"Kilgore, I'll never regret not selling to you." Gideon gritted his teeth to keep from saying more.

Kilgore guffawed as though Gideon's reply was the funniest thing he'd heard all week. "Will you regret having to board up the place and not getting a dime out of it? Think you'll be able to buy that piece of land if you don't sell this dump?" His belly shook with laughter again. The sound grated on Gideon's ears.

How did Kilgore know about the land he wanted to buy? Gideon narrowed his eyes and fixed his gaze on the pompous man. "My affairs are none of your business, Kilgore."

Kilgore pulled his cigar out of his mouth and pointed it at Gideon. "I thought you were smarter than that, but you're a fool, Maxwell. You still haven't learned that I'm the most important man in these parts. But you'll learn it now because my offer just dropped two hundred dollars."

Before Gideon could retort, both men were drawn to the sound of footsteps. Tessa stood just inside the door. Gideon saw her expression change from friendly to apprehensive the moment she laid eyes on Kilgore.

At the sight of his employee, Kilgore gave another humorless laugh. "Birds of a feather, as they say." He jerked his thumb in Tessa's direction. "I offered this girl a job making good money at the Blue Goose. You'd think she'd rather work where she could sashay around and dally with the customers, but she turned me down flat." His tone turned dramatic, laced with sarcasm. "I guess she thinks she's too good to serve whiskey. She'd rather bake bread and make half the money rather than soil her hands on demon drink." He laughed, but then the snide mockery drained from his face as he narrowed his eyes at Tessa. "She doesn't understand that I don't take no for an answer." He stuck his cigar in his mouth and took a puff. The smoke shot from his lips in a derisive jeer.

He turned to Tessa and gestured toward Gideon. "Here's just the man for you, girl. You're two of a kind. Both of you are too stupid to know a good deal when you hear one."

He flicked his ashes on the floor and walked out.

&

A flood of humiliation crashed over Tessa. Flames shot up her throat and consumed her. Bad enough Mr. Kilgore extended such a degrading offer to her in the first place, but to repeat it in front of Gideon made her wish she was invisible, especially if what Tillie and Flossie said was true. What must Gideon think of her? She couldn't even raise her eyes to look at him.

"Tessa, just ignore him. He's nothing but a windbag."

She appreciated Gideon's attempt to brush off Mr. Kilgore's crude remarks as inconsequential, but mortification still choked her. Her eyelids stung, and she bit her lip trying to halt the tears that wanted to further humiliate her. After several slow breaths, she wrangled her emotions under control.

She dared to glance at Gideon, and his warm smile sent tingles through her stomach, which only served to accuse her further. If she experienced such foolish flutters over a smile from a man she'd only known for two months, maybe she was no better than the girls Mr. Kilgore employed at the Blue Goose.

Gideon jerked his head toward the door. "Kilgore was just telling me how foolish I am for not taking his offer."

Was he trying to make her feel better by changing the subject? "What offer is that?"

Gideon pushed his shirtsleeves up higher on his arms. "He wants me to sell him the mercantile. Of course, I do want to sell, but not to him."

Tessa glanced around the store with a frown. "Why would you want to sell the mercantile? This is a good, steady business, and I'm sure you make a good living here." She pressed her lips together. It wasn't her place to make such comments.

But Gideon didn't seem to care. "My dream is to sell this place and start a ranch for breeding farm horses. Once I purchase the land and acquire my breeding stock, I'll be the only breeder in these parts."

Tessa stared at him. "My papa sold our farm to come west and dig for gold that didn't exist. It could have been a good farm, but he wanted to chase a mirage."

Gideon raised his eyebrows.

Regret niggled at her. Perhaps she shouldn't have blurted out the comparison. Regardless, she needed to complete her purchase and get back to the hotel. "I need a bar of lye soap, please."

Gideon retrieved the green paper-wrapped block and set it on the counter. "Anything else?"

She dug in her pocket for the few coins to pay for her purchase and managed a smile as she laid them on the counter. "That's all, thank you."

As she turned to leave, Gideon came around the counter. "Tessa, everyone has dreams and goals. This has been my dream for a long time. I kept the store going after my folks died so I could support my sister. Now that she's getting married, it's time for me to pursue my goal."

She looked up at him, an apology on her lips. Only days ago, she'd flirted with the idea of having her own bakery, but she'd dismissed it as foolishness. She wasn't making much money at the hotel, but at least she knew she'd receive a wage every week. After seeing what Papa put Mama through, chasing dreams left a bad taste in her mouth. "I need to get back to the kitchen. Good day, Gideon." She turned toward the door.

"Wait, Tessa. My sister and I would like you to join us for church on Sunday."

She halted. The idea sounded tempting. Mama always wanted to go to church when they lived in Indiana, but she was too weak and sickly most of the time—and of course Papa would never allow it. Whenever Tessa voiced a tentative request to attend church, Papa scoffed and told her the church folks wouldn't let the likes of her sit at worship with them. "Th–thank you, but I don't think so."

"Why not?"

The scuffed tips of her shoes drew her attention. "I don't have anything nice to wear, and besides, I'm not the kind of person that churchgoing folks associate with. But it was kind of you to ask."

Gideon kept step with her as she started toward the door. "Tessa, most of the folks in our church are farmers. Lots of them wear the same clothes to come to church that they wear to work in because that's all they have. There's nothing wrong with that."

A memory slipped through her mind. "My mama used to sing some of the church songs to me when I was little." The memory darkened. "But my father told me I could never go to a church because they don't let people like me in."

Gideon's face registered puzzled disbelief, and before he could argue the point, she beat a hasty retreat out the door.

❧

Gideon's heart ached at Tessa's reasons for refusing his invitation. He believed she wanted to go, but the image Tessa had of herself was stained with the memory of her father's ugly accusations.

He returned to the storeroom and appraised his work. Whenever he did find a buyer for the store, the bakery would only enhance its value. He decided to get started installing the stove. Surely he'd be finished well before closing time.

He measured the diameter of the section of pipe that would fit through the wall and marked the place for its installation. While he worked, he recalled the prayer he'd prayed last week, asking God to send him a wife so he could have the kind of marriage his parents had. At the time, he wondered if Tessa could be that woman, but now an element of doubt pricked him. As much as he disliked Henry Kilgore, Gideon couldn't shake the memory of the man offering Tessa a job working as a saloon girl.

"Is that what she meant when she said people like her?" His hands slowed. "God, I know I promised if You ever sent me a woman to love, I'd not question Your choice."

Gideon shook his head. He hadn't known Tessa long enough to be in love with her. Why was he even thinking in terms of love? True, he had feelings for her, but they were purely of friendship, weren't they? Isn't that why he was going to all this trouble? He felt sorry for her. Anyone else would do the same. Of course he hoped his plan would make things better for her, as well as enhance the mercantile in the eyes of a potential buyer.

"Hmm, I may run this store forever if You don't send me a buyer besides Kilgore." He immediately regretted his words and sent a repentant glance heavenward. "Sorry, Lord. I didn't mean to tell You what to do. If You want me to be a storekeeper, I'll be content to stay here for as long as You say."

He pushed the coping saw into motion. If he didn't stop woolgathering, he'd never get this job finished. He made the last cut and picked up a section of the stovepipe to test the fit. After a few more minor adjustments, he slid the section of pipe into the hole and nailed it in place. But when he began trying to connect the sections of pipe, something was wrong. Perhaps he should have connected the sections first, before installing the outside piece.

"Well, how was I to know? I've never installed a stove before." He continued muttering as he pried the nails out. Sweat trickled down his neck as he pulled the piece out and laid it on the floor with the others. He stood with his hands on his hips, glaring at the assortment of tin scattered on the floor.

"What in heaven's name are you doing?"

Gideon startled and jerked his head up.

Martha stood in the doorway, mirroring Gideon's stance with her hands on her hips and a smirk on her face.

"What's it look like I'm doing?" he snapped.

His sister pressed her lips together, and he got the distinct impression she was trying not to laugh. "Going into the scrap metal business?"

Gideon sent her a mock glower. "Think you're clever, don't you?" He spread his filthy hands and reached toward her. "Come here, and I'll show you something clever."

Martha squealed. "Ooh, Gideon, you're dirty. Don't touch me."

"Ha!" He retreated a step. "And you're going to be a farmer's wife? You'd better get used to dirt."

She made a face at him. "I was just coming to tell you that I'm going out to Ted's place. His mother and I are going to pick strawberries and make jam."

He grinned. "And you don't want Ted to see you dirty, since you'll be working in the garden and all."

Martha heaved an exasperated sigh. "Ted will bring me home later this evening, so you're on your own for supper."

"Oh, thank goodness, a reprieve."

"Gideon!"

He gave her a contrite smile. "Sorry. Have a good time, and bring me some strawberries."

After she left, a thought occurred to him. What if Tessa considered accepting Kilgore's offer of the saloon job? If Kilgore's portrayal of Tessa was accurate, he'd have no choice but to rethink the plans for the bakery. He not only had a business reputation to think of; he had a sister to protect. Despite their brother-sister banter, he adored Martha and couldn't allow her respectability to be sullied.

"I'm letting my imagination get carried away. Kilgore said Tessa turned him down flat." Besides not trusting any of Kilgore's implications, something in Gideon's heart told him Tessa simply wasn't that kind of girl.

He directed his attention back to the task at hand. These wretched sections of pipe must fit together in a particular order before he could get the whole assembly into the hole he'd cut in the wall. It appeared he might not finish this job today, and he still needed to deliver Mr. Behr's order to the hotel.

He sucked in a deep breath and blew it out. He knelt beside the collection of stovepipe pieces and tried putting sections together, but after experimenting repeatedly, they didn't fit the way he thought they should. One piece seemed too big, while another appeared too small. No matter how he attempted to join them, he always ended up with an extra length of pipe. The part he thought should fit into the wall didn't seem to fit any of the other pieces.

He didn't want to swallow his pride and ask for help, even though Cully probably knew how to put this puzzle together. He leaned against the wall and sighed his exasperation. This contraption wasn't going to get the best of him!

nine

Tessa remembered the last time someone invited her to church. It was the itinerant preacher in Indiana. Papa had run him off with a shotgun. Gideon's invitation made her heart smile even if she couldn't accept. But the fluttery sensation she got every time she laid eyes on him perplexed her. She shouldn't allow such feelings.

Grabbing a towel, she slid her pies from the oven and placed them on the cooling rack. "Who am I kidding? I get butterflies every time I *think* about him."

"Every time you think about who?"

Tessa jerked herself back to awareness and glanced over her shoulder at Flossie.

The woman's eyebrows arched in speculation.

"Oh, nobody."

Flossie laughed. "You get butterflies thinking about nobody?"

As she struggled to think how to answer, her face grew hot. Finally the stretched out silence apparently answered for her.

"Okay, I can take a hint. You don't want to talk about it."

She'd have to remember to keep her ruminations to herself. The pies cooling near the window wouldn't last through the dinner crowd, so she set to work mixing more piecrust.

As she did so, she allowed her mind to think back to Gideon's invitation. Perhaps she could wait outside the church until the service started then slip in and sit in the back. As soon as the service was over, she could slip out again before anyone noticed her.

What was she thinking? Gideon said he and his sister wanted her to join them. He must intend for her to sit with

82

them. No, she was right to refuse his invitation, regardless of how much she wanted to accept.

Tonight she planned to open Mama's Bible and read awhile. After all, that's the way she and Mama used to worship together. The only thing wrong with that plan was by the time she returned to the shed there was little or no daylight left, and she didn't have an oil lamp—or even a candle—by which to read.

28

Gideon crushed the brim of his hat in his fist as he strode down the boardwalk toward the mercantile. Something didn't add up. He'd stopped by the bank full of anticipation to learn the price and terms for the land about which he'd dreamed.

Only a few days ago Mr. Sewell seemed eager for the transaction to take place. *Why is he now telling me the land isn't for sale?* It didn't make sense for the bank to hold on to a parcel of land acquired through a defaulted loan. No, something certainly wasn't right.

He slapped his hat against his thigh as he stomped up the steps to the mercantile. The memory of Mr. Sewell repeating himself numerous times and glancing nervously at the door to an adjoining office that stood slightly ajar raised Gideon's suspicions that their conversation hadn't been entirely private.

As he propped the door open, a voice hailed him from the street.

"Gideon."

He turned. "Hey, Cully. Boy, am I glad to see you. I've been itching to get this stovepipe hooked up."

"Waall, I sure am sorry it took me so long to git here. Old man Kilgore had me puttin' new shoes on his matched team of buggy horses, and then I had to replace the wheel rims on that fancy carriage of his."

Gideon set aside his unanswered questions about Mr. Sewell's odd declaration and turned his attention to Cully and the stove. "The stove is back in the storeroom." He led the way, hoping his inability to install the contraption didn't make him look completely incompetent. If Cully could finish the job today, he could show Tessa this evening.

Cully followed Gideon and grinned at the assortment of tin pieces lined up on the floor in the corner. He picked up several pieces, scrutinizing the edges and comparing sections, tapping his finger on each piece and grunting like he was inventorying the lot. "Where's your thimble?"

Gideon raised his eyebrows. "Thimble?"

"You gotta have a thimble piece to fit these two together. Otherwise, your chimney ain't gonna be tight." Cully held up the section Gideon had nailed into the wall and then pried out. "You wasn't tryin' to nail this piece up in that hole, was ya?" Cully started to chuckle.

"Well, I was just going by the way our stove upstairs looks."

Cully's toothy grin punctuated the man's amusement. "You'd best stick to runnin' the store, Gideon. You ain't never gonna make a living installin' stoves." Cully cackled.

Gideon pressed his lips together and decided not to embarrass himself by offering to help. He set to work rearranging the displays out front.

"Hey, Gideon, what's going on?"

Gideon turned. "Mornin', Ty. What are you doing in town again? I usually don't see you more than once a month."

Ty stuck his hand deep inside the gumdrop jar. "I heard from one of the stage drivers he dropped off a guy here who might be willing to make a land deal. I came in to see if I could find him."

Gideon scratched his head. "There was a man who got off the stage the other day. Name was Behr. He mentioned something about attending to some business."

Ty chewed thoughtfully for a moment and tossed a couple more gumdrops in his mouth. "He didn't say what kind of business?"

"No, it was none of my concern. I was just happy to make a sale."

Ty nodded like it all made sense to him. "One of the stage drivers said this guy might be connected with the railroad."

"Railroad?" Gideon frowned. "I read in the paper awhile back that the Chicago, Kansas and Nebraska decided to route that connecting line about fifty miles south of here. There was some talk for a while of the Illinois Central taking over that line."

After gathering up another handful of gumdrops, Ty shrugged. "I know as much as you do. Figure I'll ask some questions and see what the answers sound like."

Gideon propped one foot on a crate of canned goods. "I had a real strange meeting today with Mr. Sewell."

"Roland Sewell at the bank?"

Gideon nodded. "You know that parcel of land east of town that I've been looking at?"

Ty arched his eyebrows and swallowed. "You finally gonna buy that piece? Hey, that's great. Nice stretch of land. A little too hilly for planting wheat and corn, but you've always wanted to breed horses. That's some mighty pretty pasture land."

Gideon scratched his head. "When I checked at the land office last week, they said the bank owned it. But today, Mr. Sewell told me it wasn't for sale. Don't you find that a little odd?"

Puzzlement drove Ty's eyebrows into a furrow. "That doesn't make sense. Why would the bank want to hold a piece of land?"

Either insight or speculation—Gideon didn't know which—fit some tentative pieces into place. "Unless. . ." He rubbed his hand over his chin and looked straight at Ty. "Are you thinking what I'm thinking?"

"Talk of the railroad coming through might drive up the price of land sky-high."

Gideon caught the corner of his lip between his teeth. "If the rumor is true, it might. When you get done talking with Mr. Behr, can you drop by and let me know what you found out?"

Ty tossed his hat on his head. "If it's anything worth passing on, you'll be the first to know."

"Thanks, buddy."

"Sure thing." Ty started for the door.

"Uh, Ty?"

"Huh?"

"That'll be four cents for the gumdrops."

"Put it on my account."

"You don't have an account."

"Oh. Well, could I open an account?"

"For four cents' worth of gumdrops?"

Ty pulled out his pocket linings and raised his shoulders, chagrin on his face.

Gideon laughed and shook his head. "Get out of here, you gumdrop thief."

"See you later."

"You better have a nickel on you when you come back."

"A nickel? You said four cents."

"I charge interest."

"Gideon, you got a catalog for stove parts?" Cully's request rang like a dirge in Gideon's ears. He pulled the catalog from underneath a shelf and pushed it across the counter to the old gent. Cully flipped through the pages and turned the book around for Gideon's perusal.

"This part right here." Cully's grimy finger tapped the page of the catalog. "You gotta have this here thimble connector, and you gotta have a collar piece before you can put that stove to work."

Gideon's shoulders slumped. Ordering parts would certainly hinder his plans. "Thanks, Cully. I'll order these parts right away."

Cully nodded and sucked on his teeth. "Sure 'nuf. See ya in church." He strolled out the door, leaving Gideon to stand in the middle of the storeroom and chafe in frustration over the delay. More than anything, he wanted to see Tessa leave Kilgore's employ and have a decent place to live.

"Just like everything else, I need to wait on God and let Him work things out."

"A sound plan, young man."

Gideon spun around to see Hubert Behr standing in the doorway. "Oh, I'm sorry. I didn't hear you come in, Mr. Behr."

"I apologize, young man. Eavesdropping is an unseemly pastime. But I must say, it's refreshing to find such wisdom in a person your age. If more people would follow God's leadership, they'd make far fewer mistakes and experience far less heartache."

Gideon followed his customer to the front of the store. "You sound like you know what you're talking about, sir."

Mr. Behr nodded slowly. "Indeed."

Gideon wiped his hands on his apron. "What can I get for you, sir?"

"I spoke with a friend of yours earlier—a young man, Mr. Ty Sawyer. He told me your general mercantile was for sale."

Gideon nodded. "Yes sir, it is."

"May I ask the price?"

The man's inquiry might mean nothing if the bank wouldn't sell the land he wanted to buy, but Gideon gave him the figure.

Mr. Behr stroked his chin. "That seems like a fair price."

Gideon watched the gentleman scan the displays of merchandise and examine the rows of bins. "Does that mean you're interested in buying the place?"

Mr. Behr ran his hand along the counter. "I need to study the feasibility of such a venture. I'll be in the area for some time, and I'm not in any hurry."

A glimmer of hope surged. Now if only he could persuade Mr. Sewell to sell him that land. . .

❧

"Flossie, do think it would be all right if I'd bring my Bible back to the kitchen tonight and read? I don't have any light at my place." Tessa hung her apron on the peg near the door as the three women were leaving.

Flossie shook her head. "That ain't a good idea. Kilgore don't like burnin' the lamps for an extra minute, the old skinflint. Iffen he sees the light burnin' and comes in here to check, he'll fire you for sure."

Disappointment slumped Tessa's shoulders, but she bid Flossie and Tillie good night and made her way out into the alley that led to her humble dwelling. Her feet came to a halt as soon as she turned the corner behind the hotel. Sitting beside the door of the shed was a small crockery vessel with a wooden lid. *Gideon.* She picked up the container and hesitated. Should she march straight to the mercantile this minute and plunk down eighteen cents? She frowned. The store was probably closed by now. Gideon was just being kind, like when he brought the burn salve to Flossie. Humility poked her. God would want her to respond in gratitude and graciousness. Very well. She'd wait and pay him for it first thing in the morning.

The moment she opened the shed door, little trespassers skittered along the wall behind Mama's cabinet. Nasty critters.

She stamped her feet and thumped her fist against the lid of the trunk. "Shoo! I'm home, you wretched little beasts. You better not have been into my food again." Her fingers groped in the cabinet to locate her bundle containing a corn muffin, an apple, and the cheese she'd purchased yesterday. Sure enough, there was another hole despite several thicknesses of paper. She touched course crumbs littering the shelf in the cabinet. The miserable rodents didn't even have the manners to clean up after themselves.

Her stomach shuddered with distaste and at the same time complained of its emptiness. The cheese, apple, and muffin were all she had. She'd simply have to break off and discard the nibbled edges. It was that or go hungry. Whatever remained after she'd eaten would be safely protected in her new crock.

After the long day of standing at the worktable and waiting on the dining customers, her body begged for rest. Despite her weariness, she'd thought about Mama's Bible all afternoon. Gideon's invitation to church kindled a spark within her to renew her fellowship with God.

If she couldn't use the kitchen lamp, perhaps there was another secluded corner where she'd find some light. The hotel lobby was for paying customers, not the likes of her. Tessa could only imagine Mr. Kilgore's reaction if he found her sitting and leisurely reading like a grand lady. But it was the only place that offered a source of lamplight in the evening.

Well, not the only place. The saloons were open, and though there was plenty of light there, the idea of sitting in a saloon made Tessa's flesh crawl. The reek of whiskey along with memories of her father's drinking habits sent shivers of loathing down her spine. Her stomach clenched at the thought of entering a saloon for any reason, even just for the purpose of taking advantage of the light.

She splashed water in her face from the bucket in the corner and ran a broken comb through her hair. If she made herself more presentable, might she dare take Mama's Bible and sit in the hotel lobby to read?

The Bible clutched under her arm, she walked down the alley toward the front of the building. When she reached the boardwalk and peered in the front window, the first person she saw was Mr. Kilgore. There was no chance of entering unnoticed.

Disappointment struck her again. Why did she think she could elevate herself to the level of the hotel patrons when she was nothing more than hired help?

She edged closer toward the front of the hotel. Perhaps there would be enough light coming from the window. She no sooner opened the book and found the broom straw she'd used to mark her place than the front door opened.

Mr. Kilgore stepped out and struck a match on the post to light his cigar.

She shrunk as close to the shadow of the building as she could. He puffed away for a moment, and the noxious smoke floated in her direction, burning her eyes and throat. She tried to hold her breath, but as the smoke slithered around her, a cough escaped despite her effort to be invisible.

"What do you think you're doing there, girl? You can't loiter around here," Mr. Kilgore's voice boomed. "Employees use the side entrance. My clientele doesn't need to see the likes of you dawdling by the front door. Run along."

The stares of passersby and Mr. Kilgore's glare gave her feet wings. The cool night air blew against her burning face as she scurried down the street. She didn't stop until she was well away from the hotel.

Tinny piano music and coarse laughter accosted her ears. Just ahead on the boardwalk, patrons of the Blue Goose saloon came and went by way of the swinging door. There was certainly plenty of light coming from those front windows. Tiptoeing inside the establishment undetected seemed as unlikely as slipping past Mr. Kilgore in the hotel lobby. The longer she stood in the shadows staring at the saloon's glow, the more she longed for a place where she could sit and read the passages Mama had underlined.

She sidled up next to the window and leaned against the

building. She'd dropped the broom straw when Mr. Kilgore bellowed at her, but she had little trouble finding her place. The page was so dog-eared and its edges so worn from use that it had to be one of Mama's favorites. The yellow glow from the window fell across the words her mother loved.

"The Lord is my strength and my shield; my heart trusted in him. . .with my song I will praise him."

Tessa doubted the discordant music coming from the saloon was the kind of song the psalmist had in mind, but she was reminded of the songs her mother taught her from the time she was a little girl. A sweet hum of memory seeped into her mind, and the words of Mama's favorite hymn caressed her heart.

"Fairest Lord Jesus, Ruler of all nature. . ."

Tessa tried to recall the rest of the words, but the noise from the saloon was so loud and distracting it was impossible to block it out. How Papa would laugh if he could see her now.

She pushed the thought from her mind. She was here to take advantage of the light. There would be time to recall those precious memories of hymn singing with Mama later. Maybe when she went to the mercantile to pay for the crock, she could also purchase a candle so she could read in the privacy of the shed. Regardless, she was determined to use this time to satisfy her hunger for worship. She read further down the page. Some of the psalms were familiar. She remembered her mother reading them to her.

"Thou art my hiding place. . . ."

The idea of God hiding her comforted her heart. She read it over again. Was a promise that precious meant for someone like her? Did she dare claim it? She closed her eyes and envisioned God covering her with His hand.

"Looky here. C'mere, little darlin'." A hand seized her arm and yanked her from her reverie. The unshaven face of a man she didn't know loomed before her. His menacing eyes swept up and down her frame. "You 'n' me's gonna have a little party, honey." His sour breath was so vile she nearly retched.

Her heart pounded, and her mouth was devoid of spit as the lecherous brute tightened his grip and pulled her toward the swinging doors. She planted her feet squarely, pulling away from the drunken man with all her strength. When she opened her mouth to protest, nothing came out except a raspy hiss.

ten

Gideon knocked on Miss Pearl's door as the crickets and cicadas were tuning up for an evening serenade. When she opened the door, Gideon noticed small, pinched lines around her eyes and a lock of gray hair that had escaped its pins.

"Hello, Gideon. Come in."

"Evening, Miss Pearl. I'm sorry to come by so late, but I needed to let you know we've run into a problem. Cully said we're missing some parts for the stove. I sent the order today and stated it was a rush order, so I'm hoping it won't take too long."

The woman brushed her hair back as she nudged Gideon toward a kitchen chair. She sliced a large piece of gingerbread and set it in front of him with a glass of milk. "I'm certainly ready for Tessa to come and take over the baking." Miss Pearl sat opposite Gideon with a cup of tea.

Gideon took a gulp of milk. "The challenge will be getting her to agree to our plan without thinking she's taking charity."

"Charity? Why, that's silly. She'll be working for her room and board by doing the baking for me. And what a blessing that will be!"

Gideon let out a rueful chuckle. "She's got a streak of pride, and that's for sure." He pressed his lips into a thin line and recalled Tessa's response when he urged her to take the food crock. He wondered if she'd found it on her doorstep yet. "She won't take anything that she can't pay for or thinks she hasn't earned."

Miss Pearl rolled her head from side to side and reached

up to massage the back of her neck. "Do you think she'd agree to move in here right away while we're waiting for the stove parts?"

Gideon forked up a piece of gingerbread and paused with the tempting morsel balanced an inch from his lips. "I'd like nothing better than to move her in here tonight. But if we have every detail of the plan in place before we present it to her, it will make it harder for her to say no." He shoveled the large bite of gingerbread in his mouth and washed it down with another swallow of cold milk.

The thought of Tessa working herself into exhaustion every day at the hotel with nothing more than a ramshackle shed to call her home troubled him more deeply than he cared to admit. Gideon shook his head. "Every time I think of her over there in Kilgore's kitchen, I could bite a horseshoe in half. I don't like the way he treats her."

"Henry Kilgore is a scoundrel, and that's a fact."

Gideon snorted and sank his teeth into the last bite of gingerbread. "I've got to get going. Martha will be wondering where I am." He rose and moved toward the door but stopped abruptly. "Say, Miss Pearl, do you have any of Maggie's kittens left?"

"They're out on the back porch. Take your pick."

He crossed the kitchen to the porch.

Three kitties curled up, overlapping each other in a basket. Maggie assumed a regal pose beside them and switched her orange and white tail while she surveyed him with aloof detachment.

Gideon scratched the top of the mother cat's head. "You have some mighty pretty babies there, Miss Maggie. Would it be okay with you if I take this one with me?" He stooped down and gently eased a sleepy white kitten with orange patches into his arms.

The kitten, which was the image of its mother, immediately

nestled against his chest.

"Much obliged, Maggie. I promise your baby will have a good home."

The mother cat craned her neck as though telling her offspring good-bye and curled up with the remaining kittens.

Gideon returned to the kitchen and held up his choice for Miss Pearl's approval.

"That one's real playful. Martha will like her."

Gideon grinned and rubbed the kitten's chin. "She's for Tessa. I hope this little one will be a good companion for her."

Miss Pearl arched an eyebrow as she walked him to the door. "Why not just leave the kitten here? Tessa will be moving in here shortly."

Gideon lifted his shoulders. "She has an urgent need for a cat's hunting abilities."

Miss Pearl shuddered and frowned. "Ooh, Gideon, we need to get her moved out of that awful shed and over here as soon as possible."

"Believe me, I wish I could convince her this very minute. I telegraphed the order and left word for the agent at the freight depot in Dubuque to notify me as soon as the parts are on their way. I'll let you know when they arrive. Thanks for the gingerbread and this little mouser." He tucked the kitten inside his shirt as he descended the stairs and headed home.

Just as he turned the corner, his attention was drawn to the boisterous activity across the street at the Blue Goose Saloon. The raucous shouting and bawdy revelry shattered what should have been a peaceful evening. His irritation mounted when he thought of the immorality taking place inside. He skewed his face into a frown. Some of that activity seemed to be spilling out onto the boardwalk. Then his feet froze in place.

Tessa? Was that Tessa out in front of the saloon? The man she was with left her and staggered back into the saloon while Tessa disappeared into the shadows, but the noise emanating from the place prevented Gideon from hearing anything they might have said to each other. The feelings he'd kept telling himself were purely friendship exploded in his chest, and something twisted in his gut. Did Kilgore convince her to take the saloon job?

ﺨ

Tessa locked her fingers around Mama's Bible and ripped her arm from the drunken oaf's grasp. Her feet flew down the alley, carrying her away from the nightmarish scene. She didn't stop until she reached the shed.

Tessa slipped inside the dark refuge, pushed the door closed, and sucked in great gulps of air. Her own heartbeat pounded so loud in her ears that she was certain the despicable man would only have to follow the sound of it to find her. Beads of cold sweat dripped down her neck and back. The skin on her wrist burned where the man's fingers had scraped when she pulled her arm from his grip. Dizziness washed over her trembling frame, and she allowed her weakened knees to buckle and lower her to the floor. Pressing her back against the door, she closed her eyes and braced her feet against the trunk.

The lingering stench of the man's sour breath smelled just like Papa's after he'd come home from town with a bottle in his hand and rage in his heart. She swallowed back the nausea the memory evoked. Uncontrollable shudders spilled over her like a bucket of icy water, and she let go of her tears.

All she'd wanted was some light by which to read Mama's Bible. Still clutched in her cramped fingers, the book flopped like a half-stuffed rag doll. Even in the darkness, she could feel the torn pages and broken spine. "Mama, I'm sorry. I should have taken better care of your Bible." Salty tears slid across her lips. Guilt over the damaged Bible hung its accusing weight around her.

She reached out to feel for the trunk's latch. Her fingers found the leather flap, and she lifted the lid, tucking the Bible inside with a heavy heart. Wrestling the trunk's bulk across the small space, she wedged it against the door.

Tomorrow's daylight would no doubt point further condemnation at her when the full measure of harm to the Bible became apparent. For now, she'd lie on her quilt and listen for staggering footsteps and a slurred voice.

☙

Darkness still hung its heavy curtain over the town, but Gideon hadn't been able to close his eyes all night except in prayer. He tiptoed in his stocking feet down the back stairs to the solitude of the mercantile.

Despite trying to deny what he saw, the fact remained Tessa was consorting with some disreputable-looking man in front of the saloon. True, she disappeared into the shadows and the man entered the saloon without her. But what if things were as they appeared?

Tessa seemed repulsed by the idea the day Kilgore blurted out his sordid offer. Either she'd been pretending, or she'd swallowed her pride and accepted the job.

Gideon raked his fingers through his hair. Two pictures tangled in his mind—one of Tessa standing in the doorway of the house he hoped to build someday and the other of Tessa outside the saloon with that man. The two couldn't be reconciled to each other. If God was going to answer his prayer for a good marriage, the Lord certainly wouldn't draw him to a fallen woman.

"God, I'm confused. Were You truly leading me to Tessa? Should I continue working on the bakery if she's made the choice to work in the saloon?"

The sign he'd finished painting yesterday lay on the shelf

in the storeroom, ready to hang in the front window of the mercantile. The cheery yellow and green letters he'd painted were now dry. TESSA'S BAKERY. When he'd spoken the words yesterday, he'd done so with excitement. Now they sounded hollow. His heart ached with the possible truth of what he'd seen.

"God, I thought maybe Tessa was the woman You've chosen for me. Maybe I was wrong. Please make things clear for me, so I can follow the path You want me to take." A verse in Psalm 5 came to mind. *"Make thy way straight before my face."*

No audible voice responded, but an unmistakable nudge moved in his heart—God's admonishment to not judge but simply wait.

Wait? All right, Father, I'll wait. Please reveal Your will to me one way or the other. I thought setting Tessa up in her own bakery was Your plan. Maybe it wasn't. I thought maybe You had chosen Tessa for me. Maybe You didn't. All I can do is wait.

"At any rate, maybe it's a good thing I found out about this before I started having real feelings for her." Incrimination prickled in his middle. Whether he admitted it or not, his heart was already drawn to Tessa.

He propped the front doors open and displayed the OPEN sign.

He spent the morning moving stock from one shelf to another, muttering as he went. Sometimes having no customers in the store was a good thing. He could talk to himself without anyone thinking he was daft. There was more than one reason a man could go loony, and he suspected most of those reasons had to do with women.

He worked his way along the shelf, until he came to his inventory of crocks, the ones with the snug lids. He picked one up and stared at it. If he felt nothing for her, why did it matter to him that she needed a vessel to keep mice out of her food? Why did the prospect of Tessa working in the saloon fill him with an ache so painful he could barely draw a breath? He returned the crock to the shelf.

"That's the problem. I do feel something for her, and the way she's living bothers me more than I can put into words." He dropped his arms to his sides. "That's not the only thing I can't put into words."

Light footsteps on the wood floor made him turn. If there was a day that he didn't want to look at those hazel eyes, this was it. The morning sun gilded her hair, turning it the color of sun-ripened wheat. She sent him a shy smile, and he nearly choked on his thoughts.

"Good morning, Gideon."

He let out the breath he was holding. "Morning."

She walked up to the counter and laid down eighteen cents. "Thank you for bringing the crock. That was very kind."

Gideon detected a hint of strained humiliation in her voice, but she didn't utter a word of anger over his deed.

"Do you sell candles?"

His tongue simply lay there, paralyzed between his teeth, and refused to function. *Answer her, you idiot, or she'll think you've lost your mind.*

At that moment he was quite certain he'd lost his heart, but God's instructions were to wait. He had a hundred questions to ask her, and he feared the answers. Impatience hammered inside his rib cage.

But in the meantime, she was standing there waiting for an answer. What was her question? "I'm sorry, what did you need?"

Tessa sent him a skeptical look. "Did I come at a bad time?"

Gideon kicked his brain into motion. "No, not at all. What can I get for you today, Tessa?"

Her brows lowered into an uncertain frown. "Candles?"

"Sure. I carry several sizes." He forced his feet in the direction of the shelf that contained the large divided tray with a variety of candles. He scooped up a handful of the most popular size. "These are two cents apiece. How many do you need?"

"Just one, please."

Gideon paused in midmotion. "One candle?"

She straightened her shoulders. "Yes, please." She laid two pennies on the counter.

"You sure that's all you need?"

She leveled her gaze straight into his eyes. The hazel eyes darkened a bit and erected a stubborn, defensive barrier. "Yes, I'm sure."

"One candle it is." He laid her purchase on the counter and picked up the pennies. "Before you go, I have a surprise for you. Wait right here." He hurried to the storeroom. As he picked up the kitten, he allowed his gaze to drift over the stove, worktable, and shelving. This would be the perfect time to show her the work he'd put into the project on her behalf. No, he needed answers to some of his questions first. And besides, God told him to wait. He returned to the front with the kitten in his arms.

The guarded look in her eyes fell away. "Oh! What a sweet kitty." She reached out and gathered the ball of orange and white fluff against her chest. "Just listen to that purr. It's like she's singing." She caressed the kitten's head, and the little cat reciprocated by rubbing against Tessa's chin. "You mean you're giving her to me? To keep?" Her eyes glistened.

"I thought she might keep you company."

Her smile put the rays of the morning sun to shame. "Oh, thank you, Gideon." She buried her nose into the kitten's silky fur. "We had barn cats back in Indiana, but Papa wouldn't let me pet them. He said their only purpose was to keep down the mouse popula. . ." The word faded on her lips, and she gave Gideon a knowing look.

"Cats are good for that, too, I suppose."

She raised her eyebrows at him. He hadn't fooled her at all. "Whatever your reason for giving her to me, thank you, Gideon." She scratched the kitty under the chin. "I think I'll name her. . .Daisy. But now I really must hurry and get back to work. I told Flossie I'd only be gone a few minutes. It's all I can do some days to keep up with all the orders for cakes and pies."

Uncertainty and impatience drove all good sense from his head. "Cakes and pies? I thought you changed jobs."

Tessa shook her head. "No, I'm still working at the hotel kitchen. Why would you think I'd gotten another job?"

Heat climbed his chest and burned its way up his neck. "I saw you—last night. In front of. . ."

Her eyes widened, and the color drained from her face. Apparently she didn't know she'd been caught.

He hated confronting her, but he had to know the truth. If her stricken expression was any indication, he must be right.

Tears filled her eyes, and she hugged the kitten close. "You saw me out in front of the saloon so you supposed that I was working there?" Mortification permeated the curves of her mouth, and fire lit her eyes.

What he first thought to be tears of shame, he now realized were tears of anger. "Well, I—"

"You what? You assumed I was the kind of girl who would take a job like that?"

"No, I—I mean, I saw you, and I—I just wondered. . . ."

"You wondered what I was doing there."

"Well, yes. Tessa, why?"

Her jaw muscle twitched, and her eyes narrowed. "Not that it's any of your business, *Mr.* Maxwell, but I was looking for some place where I could read my mother's Bible."

Gideon blinked. "Oh, so naturally you would go to the saloon to read the Bible." He couldn't keep the sarcasm from his voice. "Tessa, that makes no sense. Why would you do that?"

She sucked in a breath and blinked rapidly, but a tear escaped anyway as her voice trembled. "Mr. Kilgore wouldn't let me sit in the hotel lobby or use the lamp in the kitchen. The only other place where there was enough light to read by was the saloon. I didn't go in. I stood outside by the front window. But it was so noisy, and the men were so—so vile, I decided—" She lifted her chin. "I decided I would simply have to buy a candle so I could read in the shed." With that, she picked up her candle, snuggled the kitten onto her shoulder, turned on her heel, and marched out the door.

Gideon's voice failed him. God had directed him to wait, but instead he blurted out what was on his mind. Why couldn't he learn to listen to God's instruction? He kicked the corner of the counter and strode to the door. "Tessa! Tessa, wait!"

He caught sight of her skirt as she disappeared around the corner of the alley. He stood there staring, hoping she would come back—but she didn't. Nausea stung his throat. He owed both Tessa and God an apology.

He was about to turn to go back to the storeroom for a heartfelt talk with God when something farther down the street caught his eye. Standing out in front of the land office was Hubert Behr, and walking up to greet him was Kilgore. The two men shook hands, spoke for a moment, exchanged a piece of paper, and then stepped inside the land office together.

eleven

Tessa stormed down the alley toward the shed, huffing each breath out in rhythm with her pace. If Gideon Maxwell thought for one minute he could stand there and accuse her of being a wanton woman, he could just go soak his head in a horse trough.

She'd believed him when he said he was her friend and even felt fluttering tickles in her middle when she thought about him. The confusing ache in her heart tugged her first one way then another.

Realization swept over her. The flutters she experienced every time Gideon entered her thoughts were more than simple attraction. The comfort and warmth of being in his presence grew stronger each time she saw him. To think he assumed she was a woman of loose morals made her eyes water as surely as if he'd slapped her.

The kitten in her arms protested her tightening grip.

"I'm sorry, Daisy. I'm not angry at you." She ran a gentle caress over the kitty's head.

Daisy leaned into Tessa's stroking and purred.

Tessa scooted the kitten into the shed and closed the door. The mice were in for a surprise.

Perhaps she'd been surprised as well. Maybe Gideon wasn't the man she thought him to be.

She hastened back to the kitchen and grabbed her apron. Working would take her mind off Gideon. A basket of apples sat beside the large mixing bowl on the worktable. She thumped an apple on the table and stabbed at it, hacking it in half, then in quarters, taking pleasure in chopping the hunks into thin slices.

"What's the matter with you?"

Looking up, she found both Flossie and Tillie staring at her.

Tillie shrugged. "You seem kinda moody. Something wrong?"

Gideon's question rang in her ears. *"Why would you do that?"* Yes, there was something wrong, but she forced a smile and shook her head. "I'm thinking about adding a buttermilk spice cake to tomorrow's menu."

Flossie wasn't fooled. "Is that what you went to the mercantile to talk to Gideon Maxwell about? Spice cakes?"

Tessa riveted her eyes on her task as she continued to slice the apples. "What would Gideon Maxwell know about dessert menus?" *What does Gideon Maxwell know about anything?* "I was also thinking about making a peach cobbler. Can we get peaches from any of the local farmers?"

"You can buy canned peaches at the mercantile."

Tessa tightened her grip on the handle of the knife. "I'd rather use fresh." She pushed the blade of the knife through the apples with increased energy.

Flossie reached out and patted her shoulder. "Whatever's wrong between you two, you need to talk it out."

The apple slipped from Tessa's hand, and the knife took a tiny nick from her finger. She sucked in a breath. "I don't know what you're talking about." She stuck her finger in her mouth.

"Yes, you do. You were happy as a lark when you left here. You came back with fire in your eyes. What happened?"

Tessa examined her finger. Not much damage. On the other hand, her heart was bleeding. How foolish to allow herself to daydream about a man like Gideon. Hadn't Papa always told her not to get any highfalutin ideas about attracting the attention of an upstanding man? She could still hear his bitter laughter when he told her she might as well fall in love with one of the pigs.

Fall in love? The notion of love was a will-o'-the-wisp. Nothing there to grasp and hold. Oh, how she wished she could talk to Mama.

Tears burned the inside of her eyelids, and she stiffened her spine. Daydreams might be fine for schoolgirls, but she had a job to do. Swallowing hard, she picked up another apple and quartered it.

Flossie still waited for an answer.

"Nothing worth talking about, and I need to get these pies in the oven."

❧

By two o'clock the lunch crowd dwindled. Tessa began clearing dirty dishes and changing table linens in the dining room.

Mr. Kilgore walked in with a man whom she remembered seeing once or twice.

Tessa did her best to avoid following the pair with her eyes. Her face still heated when she remembered the way Mr. Kilgore embarrassed her in front of Gideon. Not that it mattered anymore. Gideon already thought the worst of her.

"Tessa! Bring coffee for myself and Mr. Behr to my office."

Hurrying to do his bidding, she set cups and a coffeepot on a clean tray with spoons, cream, and sugar. She carried the tray to the back of the dining room where the door to the office stood open and deposited it on the small table beside the gleaming mahogany desk.

Not wishing to linger in Mr. Kilgore's presence any longer than necessary, she poured the coffee and returned to the dining room to finish cleaning. The tables along the back wall all needed to be cleared and she couldn't help hearing snatches of the men's conversation as Mr. Kilgore's voice carried into the quiet of the nearly empty dining room.

"I understand you've made inquires about purchasing property in this area."

The other man's reply was drowned out as Tessa stacked dishes on her tray, but a few disjointed words pulled her senses to attention.

"...young man...Maxwell's Mercantile..."

Mr. Kilgore's booming laughter rang out. "Gideon Maxwell is a fool. I already offered to buy that place of his, and he turned me down. You'd think he'd want to unload it."

Tessa continued to stack dirty plates and coffee cups, ashamed for listening but wide-eyed at Mr. Kilgore's remarks about Gideon. Taking more time than necessary for her chore, she straightened chairs and tablecloths. Mr. Kilgore wasn't making any effort to lower his voice. Was it wrong to tarry and hear more words that weren't meant for her ears?

"I already own several businesses in town." Kilgore's pompous tone irritated her. "I'm putting pressure on Jake Peabody who owns the gristmill. It won't be long before I own that enterprise as well. The Standridge brothers own the sawmill, but I don't think they'll give me too much trouble about selling out. Maxwell is the only nut I haven't been able to crack."

Tessa heard the sound of fingers drumming on the desktop, and the other man cleared his throat. "I see. Seems to me that you've already acquired a rather substantial portion of the town."

One of the men took a noisy slurp of coffee.

"Not only the town, Mr. Behr, but also some of the outlying areas. I have some inside sources who keep me apprised on..." He cleared his throat. "Well, let's just say I have access to certain opportunities. Of course you're privy to much of the same information—maybe even more so—working for the railroad as you do."

"It's true that I'm privy to a great many things, Mr. Kilgore. Some things may surprise you."

Mr. Kilgore's chuckle rang wickedly in her ears. "Ah, Mr. Behr, that is precisely why I felt it might be advantageous for us to form a partnership." A chair squeaked. "I've already begun to make some strategic moves, but with the information you can provide, we could triple our assets by this time next year."

"Strategic moves?"

"You know that young man you were talking about, Gideon Maxwell? I happen to know he wants to buy a piece of land east of town. He's been downright pigheaded over refusing to sell the mercantile to me, so I bought that piece of land myself. Now, if he wants it, he'll have no choice but to sell me the mercantile first. Then, if he wants that land, he'll have to match the railroad's price, and he doesn't stand a chance of being able to do that. Not only will I have that prime stretch of land, but I'll have the mercantile as well."

There was a pause. Tessa heard clicking china. She wished she could see the faces of the men.

"Competition between land speculators is fierce, as you well know, Mr. Behr. A few creative adjustments of the survey maps will put us at a great advantage when it comes time for the contracts to be signed. In addition, business owners stand to turn a tidy profit by—shall we say—*unofficial* agreements with the railroad."

When the man named Behr finally replied, it sent a shiver down her spine. "Very shrewd, Mr. Kilgore. Very shrewd, indeed."

Tessa started to pick up her loaded tray when a water glass slid and tumbled to the floor.

A moment after the crash, Mr. Kilgore appeared in the doorway. "What's this? What are you doing, girl?"

Tessa caught her lip between her teeth as she stooped to pick up the shards of broken glass. A rush of blood filled her face with heat. "I'm sorry, Mr. Kilgore. I was just cleaning these tables and dropped a glass."

She didn't dare look up. It wasn't like she set out to eavesdrop on his conversation, but she didn't hasten to move out of earshot either. The pieces of broken glass jiggled in her trembling hand.

"This will come out of your pay! Now get this mess cleaned up." He stomped back into his office and slammed the door.

Relief wilted her shoulders. If he suspected her of listening to his conversation with Mr. Behr, he didn't let on. More than happy to comply with his orders, she hoisted her burden of dirty dishes and carried them to the kitchen.

Safely within the walls of the kitchen, she deposited the dishes by the sink and returned to her worktable. As she assembled the ingredients for tomorrow's spice cakes, Mr. Kilgore's words came back to her. Did Gideon know Mr. Kilgore had purchased the land he wanted? Her boss's other statements regarding the railroad made no sense to her, but the arrogance in his voice raised the hackles on her neck. It didn't take a Philadelphia lawyer to figure out that her employer was up to something unscrupulous. Now she had one more reason to dislike the man.

While she measured flour and spices into her mixing bowl, she entertained the inclination to go and tell Gideon what she'd heard. Conflicting notions collided in her head. Yes, she had feelings for Gideon. If she didn't, his reproachful questions wouldn't have hurt so much. On the other hand, uneasiness over what she'd heard made her wish she could run to the mercantile this minute and tell Gideon. But repeating information not meant for her ears was as unethical as eavesdropping. Why add to Gideon's low opinion of her?

Anger welled in her stomach. She'd let her attraction to Gideon grow, and he'd stepped on it and ground it into the dust. No good could come of seeing Gideon right now, much less talking to him. She clenched her teeth, realizing the anger she felt wasn't aimed solely at Gideon. Irritation crawled up from her gut, and she resented her own fickleness.

Just forget about it. There's nothing you can do.

Forgetting about Gideon, however, wasn't so easy. Despite her every effort to resist thinking of him, he still appeared in her mind's eye. The look on his face when she stormed out of the mercantile stayed with her as she poured the cake batter into pans and slid them into the oven. What exactly was that look? Disappointment? Suspicion? Gideon's expression didn't look anything like the accusation she'd been accustomed to seeing in Papa's eyes. Was it possible what she saw was regret?

Gideon's own words indicted him. *"If you want to have a friend, you have to be a friend."* She'd not had many friends in her lifetime, hardly even one if she didn't count Mama. But she knew enough to understand that friends didn't believe untruths about each other based only on appearances.

What hurt most was the growing realization that she already regarded Gideon as more than just a friend.

❧

Daisy purred and rubbed against her ankles when Tessa opened the door of the shed. No scurrying sound fell on her ears upon her arrival.

The day's tension lifted as she picked up the little cat and rubbed its whiskers against her cheek. "I brought you a little bit of milk. Flossie said it would start to sour by tomorrow anyway."

She set Daisy down with the saucer of milk and smiled as the kitten cautiously sniffed it, took a few tentative laps, and then ignored the offering.

"I know it's not your mama's milk, but it's the best I can do." She glanced around the shed wondering if Daisy had encountered any of her roommates. Maybe they'd spread the news to all their rodent relatives that a cat now resided here.

Placing the folded quilt beside the trunk, she created a place where she could sit and have her supper. She unwrapped the cold biscuit and small bit of sausage she'd brought home and retrieved the remainder of the crackers and cheese stored in the crock. She thanked God for her meal, then she broke off a piece of cheese and popped it into her mouth along with a nibble of sausage.

As the rich flavors satisfied her hunger, she watched Daisy play with a corner of the quilt. Despite the strain of her day, she couldn't help smiling at the kitten's fierce little growls as she pounced on some imaginary prey. Then she realized Daisy had some kind of object between her paws.

Leaning over to get a closer look, Tessa's mouth dropped open with horror. Daisy's plaything was a mouse's tail. "No wonder you weren't hungry for milk. Your belly is full of. . . mouse!"

Tessa lost her appetite and tucked the rest of her meal away in the crock. With the edge of her shoe, she shoved the bodiless tail out the door with a shiver. "I know, Daisy, you're just doing your job." It was a good thing, she supposed, but somehow the kitten lost some of her innocence and took on the aura of a miniature predator.

As the shadows engulfed the shed, she lit her candle. A cracked coffee cup served as her candle holder. She held the candle aloft to search every corner of the shed for other remains of Daisy's lunch. Finding none, she breathed a sigh of relief and sat down on the quilt with Mama's Bible.

Instead of the Psalms tonight, she turned to the New Testament and began leafing through the pages, reading an underlined verse here or there. The marks showed her the words Mama read and loved then left as a legacy to her.

"Words to live by, honey girl. You can always trust the words in God's Book."

Tears welled in her eyes. If only Mama were here to answer some of the questions taunting her.

She turned a few more pages and found a folded bit of newspaper with torn edges. She carefully unfolded the yellowed paper and held it close to the candlelight to read the date. *"August 12, 1866."* Three days before her fourth birthday.

The article described the arrest of three men in Madisonville, Kentucky. One of the men stood accused of murder while the other two claimed to know nothing about it. Since they were in the company of the guilty man, it was at first assumed they, too, were guilty. During the trial, evidence proved the other two men innocent of the murder but suspected in various petty crimes. One of those two men had escaped custody before the verdict could be pronounced, and the name of the escapee caused her blood to freeze. "Doyle Langford." *Papa?*

She looked at the pages in First Thessalonians where Mama had tucked the scrap of newspaper. There was a verse underlined. *"Abstain from all appearance of evil."* Accompanying the verse was a dried smudge that appeared to be a water droplet. Or a teardrop.

"If Papa hadn't associated with the guilty man, he wouldn't have appeared guilty and would've had no reason to run."

Tessa's hand aimlessly stroked Daisy's fur. Being in the wrong place with the wrong person had brought suspicion down on Papa and heartache to her mother. In the candle's glow, she read the verse following the one Mama had underlined. Paul, the writer of First Thessalonians, prayed for the people he loved to remain blameless.

Tessa leaned back and closed her eyes. Had she done the very thing Papa did? By standing out in front of the saloon, she'd placed herself in the position of appearing guilty. Maybe Gideon's question wasn't one of reproach at all, but rather one of sorrow.

twelve

Gideon stared over the top of his coffee mug. "Maybe she'll come into the mercantile today," he muttered aloud. Would speaking the words make them so?

"Did you say something?"

He turned to see Martha at the sink looking at him over her shoulder. She was probably afraid he'd bite her head off again like he'd done yesterday. They'd teased each other throughout their childhood, but the past several days, even Martha tiptoed around him.

"No, nothing important."

Martha wiped her hands on a towel and crossed the kitchen to sit at the table with him. "Gideon, just go and talk to her. What's stopping you?"

When had his little sister become so intuitive? He was the big brother. She was supposed to come to him for advice, not the other way around. But he'd certainly made a mess of things where Tessa was concerned. Maybe Martha was wiser in matters of the heart. Either that or she'd simply had enough of his grumpy disposition.

He set his cup down and leaned on his elbows. "It's not that easy, honey. I said something I shouldn't have, and now I don't know how to make it right."

Martha's eyebrows arched a little. " 'I'm sorry' usually works well. And if it's your pride that's keeping you from apologizing, remember living with nothing but your pride can be awfully lonely."

Oh, being wrong was tough, especially when one's little sister pointed out the obvious. A week's worth of loneliness grated on him with relentless condemnation.

His reasoning sounded completely logical to him: He couldn't leave the store. There wasn't enough privacy to talk at the hotel. Besides, the last time he spent a few minutes talking to her while she was working, she almost got fired. Going to speak to her after work at her little dwelling wouldn't be appropriate since it was located in a back alley. All those points made perfectly good sense during the day. But at night, as he fought with the bedcovers, the feeble excuses tormented him, and there was no one to blame except the man whose face peered back at him from the mirror every morning.

Martha rose and brushed a kiss on his cheek. "Don't wait too long, Gideon. The longer you put it off, the harder it will be. And from what you've told me about her, Tessa's a nice girl." She picked up her towel. "You're going to a great deal of trouble downstairs in the storeroom to give Tessa a place to work for herself instead of for Henry Kilgore. I don't suppose you were doing all that work just to pass the time."

Gideon leaned back in his chair, pressed his lips together, and narrowed his eyes. He was about to tell her to mind her own business when she sealed her case.

"I'm sure after you've prayed about it God will tell you what to do." She patted his shoulder and returned to the breakfast dishes.

How was he supposed to refute that? He stared into his coffee cup. Sure, he'd prayed about it. He prayed God would bring Tessa into the mercantile so they could talk. But she hadn't come in—not for a whole week—and he was beginning to get the idea God wasn't going to bring Tessa anywhere. Like Martha said, he just needed to go talk to her.

"But I don't know what to say to her," he mumbled under his breath. "I wounded her. She probably never wants to see my face again." He stood and scraped his chair back across the wooden floor, continuing to mutter as he descended the squeaky stairs to the store. "She was beginning to trust me, and I hurt her."

"You aren't the one she is supposed to trust."

He halted in midstep. "God, You must get awfully tired of me trying to handle things on my own."

He stepped inside the storeroom and knelt by the work-table he'd built for Tessa. "Father, I told Martha I didn't know how to make things right between Tessa and me, but that wasn't true. I know I owe Tessa an apology. I just don't know how to make it happen. I owe You an apology, too, Lord. You've nudged me in Tessa's direction, and if I'd listened to You, maybe I wouldn't have said those stupid things. I doubted You, Father, and I didn't wait like You told me to do. Forgive me, and please work it out so I can talk to her today."

☙

Business remained slow most of the morning, giving Gideon plenty of time to carry on a running conversation with God. Now, as he scowled at the paper in his hand, he had to admit God certainly had interesting ways to test his perseverance. Not that he was complaining. He'd simply have to exercise some faith and trust.

The bell jingled announcing the arrival of a customer.

A surge of hope quickened his pulse. *Tessa?* He looked up, but it was Pearl Dunnigan's sunny smile that greeted him.

"Good morning, Gideon."

His shoulders sagged in disappointment, and he mumbled, "Morning, Miss Pearl."

The woman chuckled. "What kind of welcome is that? Should I go back out and come in again?"

Gideon sent her an apologetic smile. "Sorry." He held up the paper. "The stove parts have been shipped."

"Wonderful. How soon before they get here?"

Gideon sighed. "That will depend on how soon I can go get them."

Miss Pearl frowned. "They're not coming here?"

Gideon handed her the telegram. "I wired the freight office in Dubuque to see if the parts had come in. They've arrived, but the next shipment for this area isn't due for another week and a half. I can get there and back in three days on horseback."

She looked over the missive and returned it to him. "Who would run the store?"

"Martha. She's worked in the store plenty of times along with Pa and me. She can do it for three days." He shrugged. "I'd like to get those parts as soon as possible. Even so, it may all be for naught."

"Why, Gideon? Didn't Tessa like the idea?"

Gideon pulled the pencil from behind his ear and thumped it on the counter. "I haven't had a chance to show it to her yet. Miss Pearl, I've really messed things up."

Miss Pearl arched her eyebrows. "You want to tell me about it?"

By the time he finished the whole story, she stood with arms folded, tapping her foot. "Gideon Maxwell, you should be ashamed of yourself."

"Oh, I am."

"I'm appalled that you've let an entire week go by without going to apologize. And you're waiting for God to simply do your bidding and bring Tessa to you?"

"But Miss Pearl, it's not—"

"How do you think that poor girl felt when you asked her if she was working at that awful place?"

"I didn't mean—"

"I know your pa taught you better than that."

"Miss Pearl, I—"

"If you don't march yourself over there this minute and talk to her, I'll go myself and bring her back here with me!" Miss Pearl ended her declaration with a snort and her hands on her hips. "Well?"

Gideon took in a breath and held it for a moment. Maybe Miss Pearl had something there. At any rate, Tessa would likely be more receptive to Miss Pearl than to him at the moment.

He reached out and took Miss Pearl's hands in his. "I think that's a wonderful idea. When are you going?"

✧

Tessa stood with her mouth agape, staring at the stove and the work space in Gideon's storeroom.

Large mixing bowls, baking pans, pie plates, and utensils lined the sturdy table. Sacks of flour and sugar crowded under the table while spice tins occupied one of the shelves. The stove sat proudly in the corner, polished and waiting.

She shook her head. "Gideon, I can't do this. You know I don't have the money to pay you for these things."

She watched Gideon glance at Miss Pearl who stood to one side. The woman smiled and nodded, and he took a deep breath like he was preparing to plunge headfirst into a rain barrel.

"Tessa, it's a business arrangement. You sell your baked goods out of the mercantile, and I get a small percentage until the cost of the materials and equipment is met. After that, your only expense would be your baking supplies. In addition, you supply Miss Pearl here with baked goods for the boardinghouse in exchange for your room and board. Not only can you quit your job at the hotel and work here full-time, you'll have a pleasant place to live."

Her mind staggered in an attempt to fully comprehend all Gideon had done on her behalf. Business arrangement or not, he'd gone to a great deal of trouble, and she only had one question.

"Why?"

His hopeful expression drooped. "Why? Well, because. . . you. . .you're. . ." His shoulders rose and fell.

She remembered the only other time she saw him so befuddled and speechless was a week ago when she stormed out the door. This simply didn't make sense in the light of his earlier assumption that she'd taken the saloon job. "Gideon, I don't understand why you would go to so much trouble for someone like me."

A grimace distorted his features. "Tessa—" He seemed to forget about Miss Pearl as he took a step closer. "Tessa, this might come as a surprise to you, but it shouldn't. I care about you. I care what happens to you, and I care how you're treated. You're a lady deserving of respect."

He fidgeted a moment, staring at the floor. "Tessa, the other day when I jumped to conclusions—I was wrong." He looked up and locked his gaze on her face. "I should've known you'd never do something like that. I apologize for even considering the possibility. Please forgive me."

Forgive? Gideon was asking for her forgiveness? It was too much to take in, and she turned toward the worktable. Of all the men she'd ever known or come in contact with—Papa, Mr. Kilgore, the hotel desk clerk, even the awful man outside the saloon—Gideon was the last man she believed needed to ask for forgiveness. Her gaze traveled over the equipment, the baking supplies, and the stove.

"Tessa, please?"

She pulled her attention back to the man standing before her. His eyes remained fixed on her as if willing her to accept his declaration. She believed he was truly sorry for the misunderstanding, but she couldn't let Gideon shoulder all the responsibility.

She glanced over at Miss Pearl who, judging by her smug though teary-eyed smile, was enjoying every minute of this.

But Tessa had to clear up one thing. "There's something I have to say."

The anticipation etched on his face faded, but he didn't interrupt her.

"I found a verse underlined in my mother's Bible that says, *'Abstain from all appearance of evil.'* If I had used better judgment, I would never have gone near the saloon for any reason. And if I hadn't been there, you wouldn't have drawn the wrong conclusion. So I'm sorry, too."

Tenderness spread across Gideon's countenance.

Her guarded hesitation melted away, and a slow smile crept into her face. Did she dare allow herself to hope?

"Ahem." Miss Pearl stepped forward. "Does this mean I have a new boarder?"

How did one say thank you for such generosity and kindness? "I just can't believe you did all this—for me." She couldn't keep the tremor from her voice.

Miss Pearl patted her hand. "For us, dear. You're helping me by doing the baking. I'm getting too old to stand in the kitchen all day. And you'll be helping Gideon by bringing more customers into his store."

She liked that idea. If she could repay Gideon for all the kindness he'd offered her, then it would be easy to agree to the arrangement. "It sounds like I'll benefit more than either of you. But if you truly want a three-way partnership, then my answer is yes."

Gideon pulled a small painted sign from a shelf and held it up for her approval.

"TESSA'S BAKERY. Oh my goodness!" She clapped her hands.

"There's just one small delay." Gideon crossed the space and pointed out an area on the stove and chimney, explaining that two connecting pieces were missing. "The parts are in Dubuque. I'm leaving first thing in the morning to go get them."

Tessa nodded, still barely able to take it all in.

Miss Pearl slipped her arm through Tessa's. "Since you'll be using my kitchen to do the baking for the boardinghouse, I'd like for you to move in today, if that's all right with you."

Tessa gave the woman an impulsive hug. Her throat was too tight for any other reply.

Miss Pearl beamed. "Gideon, can you help Tessa move her things to the boardinghouse this evening?"

He gave her a silly, schoolboy grin. "My pleasure."

❧

Gideon loaded Tessa's trunk onto Cully's old wheelbarrow and dusted his hands on his pants. "Is that everything?"

Tessa stepped out the door of the shed with the kitten in her arms. Her smile set Gideon's heart tumbling. "Everything except Daisy."

He reached out and scratched the cat behind the ears. "You want to put her in the trunk?"

"Of course not," Tessa sputtered. She threw a defensive look at him and broke into a giggle at his teasing grin. "I'll just leave her in the shed, and as soon as I've finished talking to Mr. Kilgore, I'll come and get her."

The mention of Kilgore's name dampened the anticipation that had been skittering through Gideon's middle all day. "Do you want me to come with you?"

She shook her head. "No. You go ahead to Miss Pearl's with those things. This won't take long, and I'll meet you over there."

Doubt nipped at Gideon. If he knew Kilgore, the man would do his best to intimidate her. Gideon wanted to insist on accompanying her, but her independent spirit waved like a flag on the Fourth of July. "All right. But if you don't show up at Miss Pearl's place in a few minutes, I'm going to come looking for you."

The moment he arrived at Miss Pearl's back door, the

woman bustled about, directing him to carry Tessa's things to a small but clean room just off the kitchen.

"This quilt has always reminded me of spring flowers," she said as she smoothed the cover over the bed. "I hope Tessa likes it." Miss Pearl fluffed up the pillow and straightened the rag rug on the floor.

Gideon nodded. The room was a startling contrast to the dismal shed. He set down the last of Tessa's belongings and left Miss Pearl to fuss over her preparations. As he descended the back porch steps, he caught sight of Tessa coming through the shadows.

She smiled a greeting and deposited Daisy on the porch. "Thank you, Gideon, for carrying my things."

"It was my pleasure. Did Kilgore give you a hard time?"

A tight-lipped smile tugged a dimple into her face. "He told me I couldn't quit because I was fired. Again."

He could only imagine the pompous man's bluster. "Either way, you don't have to deal with him anymore."

"Thanks to you."

The evening breeze lifted sandy strands of hair across her cheek, and an unseen hand pressed him a step closer. His fingers took on a mind of their own as they reached to brush the wisp of hair from her face. She raised widened eyes to his, and his heart rolled over in his chest. Twilight's fading rays fell across her, casting bronzed reflections in her eyes. Muted sounds of the evening hushed as he focused his gaze on her lips. The blood rushed in his ears. He gently cupped her chin and started to lower his face to hers.

When his lips were mere inches from hers, she turned her head and pulled back. "Thank you again, Gideon. For everything. Miss Pearl must be waiting for me." She darted like a scared rabbit up the porch steps and through the door.

thirteen

Tessa couldn't stop staring at the cozy, cheerful room that was her new home. It wasn't much larger than the shed, but the difference made her feel as though she'd just been released from a dungeon to live in the king's palace. The blue flowers on the pitcher and basin reminded her of the blue in Mama's eyes, and the colorful quilt smelled of fresh lavender. A crisp white curtain hung at the small window.

Miss Pearl stood in the doorway. "I hope it's not too cramped, dear."

"Oh no, ma'am. It's. . .it's. . ." Her eyes traveled around the space until they came to rest on the oil lamp on the small dresser. "It's wonderful." She crossed the room and touched the sparkling glass globe of the lamp. "May I really use this?"

Miss Pearl laughed. "Of course, dear. There's a box of wood matches in the top drawer of your dresser. Now, you must be tired, so I'll leave you to get settled."

Tessa thanked her and eased down on the bed, relishing its softness. She wondered if she'd be able to sleep on a comfortable bed after sleeping on nothing but her tattered quilt on the hard ground for so long. She looked forward to finding out.

There weren't many things in her trunk or cabinet to tuck away or hang, but she extracted each item and smoothed it with her hands before giving it a home on one of the wooden pegs or a dresser drawer. She reached into the cabinet and pulled out the cracked coffee mug that served as her candle holder. The pitiful short stub of melted wax in the bottom of the cup was no longer needed now that she could sit and read by lamplight.

As she pushed the nearly empty trunk to the foot of the bed, the memory of Gideon touching her face crossed her mind like a web of silken threads. The touch of his fingers against her cheek sent flutters through her stomach. She could still feel his breath on her face.

She closed her eyes and tried to imagine how it might have felt if she'd not turned her head. Gideon's face lowering to hers caught her completely off guard. It never occurred to her that he might wish to kiss her.

"Why did I pull away from him?" No answer was forthcoming. "I wonder what was going through his mind." One thing was certain: She couldn't begin to describe what was going through hers.

❧

Tessa lay awake half the night tussling with worrisome thoughts. Her new bed was comfortable enough to invite sleep, but nagging images of Gideon loomed every time she closed her eyes. His tender expression and gentle touch lingered softly in her mind—like a melody she didn't want to forget. But her response to his touch drove her brow into a furrowed frown.

When she finally drifted off, she startled awake what seemed like only a moment later. The conversation she'd overheard between Mr. Kilgore and Mr. Behr prodded her conscience. She'd fretted all week, wondering whether or not she should tell Gideon what she'd heard. But then she'd have to admit to eavesdropping. She'd almost made up her mind to tell him last night when he carried her belongings to the boardinghouse. When he leaned down, appearing like he intended to kiss her, everything flew right out of her head. She hadn't given the overheard conversation another thought until now.

Giving up on sleep, she rose, dressed, and padded softly to the kitchen to stoke the fire in the cookstove. By the time Miss Pearl joined her, the fragrance of cinnamon spice coffee cake, fluffy biscuits, bacon, and coffee filled the air.

After the boarders finished their breakfasts, Tessa went to work kneading bread dough and setting it to rise. Later that morning, two warm, fresh loaves sat side by side and Tessa was taking cookies from the oven.

"I feel positively lazy!" Miss Pearl declared with a chuckle as she entered the kitchen.

Tessa hoisted a basket of apples to the worktable. "I thought I'd make an apple cobbler for dessert." She pushed a plate of cookies in Miss Pearl's direction. "Would you like some warm sugar cookies with your tea?"

"Mercy sakes, you're going to spoil me, child."

Tessa gave Miss Pearl a shy smile. "I'd like to spoil you. It's just my way of saying thank you."

Miss Pearl patted Tessa's shoulder. "Now, I haven't done a thing. It's all Gideon's doing." She picked up an empty basket from the pantry. "I'm going to pick some green beans from the garden." The woman stepped out the back door, leaving Tessa to work in solitude.

All Gideon's doing. The very mention of his name set her stomach to quivering. She wondered where he was now, how close to Dubuque and how soon to return.

Her unsettled heart pulled her first one way and then another when she invited last night's memory back to her mind. When Gideon's lips were inches from hers, she'd felt unable to draw a breath. His nearness paralyzed her, like time had stopped. When she'd escaped to the safety of her room and leaned against the closed door with her heart pounding in her ears, her legs barely held her up. Even now, as she recalled the touch of his fingers on her face, a shiver danced through her.

But why? Was it fear? Or something else?

When the drunken man outside the saloon grabbed her wrist that awful night, a nauseous, dreadful fear caused her to tremble. Gideon's touch was completely opposite.

"Why did I turn away from him?" Her own whisper accused her of being fickle. Her eyelids stung. She longed to talk to Mama. Miss Pearl was a sweet lady, but Tessa feared she didn't know the woman well enough to confide in her yet. Mama always knew her heart and could help her sort out her tumultuous emotions. To whom would she run now?

One of the psalms she'd read last night said God was a Father to the fatherless. The concept was almost too precious to ponder. If she claimed it, did that mean she could talk to Him when she was confused or lonely? Right now, she was both.

"God?"

She paused to gather all her tumbled thoughts.

"God, I don't know how to explain this, but I guess that's silly. I don't have to explain anything to You." She closed her eyes and sighed. "I'm so mixed up inside. Sometimes I want so badly to be close to Gideon that I ache. But when he's near, my heart feels like it's going to jump out of my chest, my hands won't be still, and all I want to do is run away."

She'd hoped speaking the words might help put her unruly emotions into perspective, but instead her own voice sounded hollow and her plea directionless. All she could do was pray God understood.

Daisy came tiptoeing into the kitchen with her tail held straight up like a tiny, furry flagpole.

Tessa scooped her up and sat on one of the kitchen chairs, settling the kitten in her lap. A twinge of envy pricked her. "God, sometimes I wish I could curl up in Your lap."

Daisy purred and kneaded her paws into the folds of Tessa's apron.

"What if I hurt Gideon's feelings last night?" Her heart spun like a whirlwind. "He's been so good and kind I can't stand thinking I might have offended him. But what I feel for Gideon isn't just because he's good and kind."

She looked out the window, beyond the yard, and through the trees. The distant hillside was dotted with headstones and makeshift crosses. Mama rested there.

"God, I don't know what to do. Help me understand. When I was a little girl and I was hurt or angry—or I couldn't understand why things were the way they were—I could always talk to Mama." Tears slipped down her face. "She helped me sort out my confusion when nothing in the world made sense. I wish she could tell me what to do about my feelings for Gideon."

She stroked the purring kitten in her lap, and Daisy pressed her head against Tessa's hand in a gesture of unfeigned love and complete trust. It reminded her of the times she'd spent as a little girl snuggled beside her mother.

"God is our refuge and our sanctuary, honey girl."

As a child, she hadn't known what those words meant. Maturing into adulthood, she walked the paths of adversity, grief, doubt, and confusion. When she found herself alone, the promises in God's Word offered sweet assurance that she could run to Him for sanctuary and comfort.

She lifted her face toward heaven. "God. . .Father. . .I love You."

❧

Tessa glanced at the clock ticking away on the parlor mantle. Two fifteen. Plenty of time to run to the mercantile for a few things.

She slipped into her room to wash her face and tidy her hair. Her appearance in the small mirror over the washstand disturbed her. Since she no longer needed to save her money to pay rent for the winter, perhaps she could purchase a new hair ribbon or even a bit of lace to add to her collar. Such an extravagance might take some getting used to.

It wasn't hard to find Miss Pearl. The woman's humming could be heard coming from the front porch where Tessa found her sweeping.

"Miss Pearl, I'm going to the mercantile. Is there anything you need?"

Miss Pearl's broom halted as the woman placed a finger on her chin. "Yes, I need some laundry blue and a couple of pounds of coffee. Tell Martha to put it on my account. And if there is anything you need for your baking here, put that on my account as well."

Tessa hesitated a moment. "I thought I'd make a ginger-bread cake for tomorrow if that would suit you. But I'll need some ginger and nutmeg."

"Gingerbread cake is one of my favorites—and Gideon's, too. Go ahead and get the spices, dear, and anything else you think we might need for the next few days." The woman resumed her sweeping and humming.

Tessa patted her pocket to ensure her own money was safely tucked away before stepping down the cobblestone walkway that led to the white picket gate. She might even purchase a hair clasp if it wasn't too costly.

The mercantile was a pleasant walk down the shady street and around the corner. Miss Pearl had told her of a shortcut through the back alley, but it was such a beautiful day that she had no desire to cut her errand short.

The house on the corner had hollyhocks growing beside the porch. The deep pinks drew her attention. She wondered if Gideon would find a hair ribbon that color becoming on her.

She turned the corner and proceeded down the main street through town. Just ahead, a door opened and a man exited an office. Tessa slowed her steps. The man had his back to her, but she still recognized Mr. Behr. He appeared to be speaking to someone behind him still inside. When the other person followed Mr. Behr onto the boardwalk, Tessa halted. She had no desire for a confrontation with Mr. Kilgore, given his ugly parting words to her the previous evening. The alley that bordered the building the two men exited provided a place for her to slip behind a stack of crates. She pressed her back against the wood-sided wall and waited for the men to pass. But they didn't pass by. They stopped right at the entrance of the alley, not ten feet from where she stood. Tessa peeked through the slatted sides of the crates that concealed her.

The sound of Mr. Kilgore's voice sent prickles up her arms. "I can assure you the Standridge brothers will see things my way. Once the sawmill is ours, the only other enterprise we lack is Maxwell's Mercantile."

"You're so certain of your persuasion with both brothers Standridge?"

A mirthless chuckle preceded Mr. Kilgore's reply. "Every man has his price, Mr. Behr. Ben and Earl Standridge both resent splitting their profits with each other. Once I convince each of them separately that his brother intends to sell his portion of the sawmill, it will just be a simple matter of drawing up a bill of sale. We'll take over that business for a fraction of what it's worth. Taking ownership of the sawmill will give us the advantage with the land speculators."

Mr. Behr stood stroking his beard.

Tessa sucked in a slow, silent breath and held it. Neither man looked in her direction, but the guilt that plagued her earlier over listening to the men's conversation at the hotel now swelled with each passing moment.

"And young Mr. Maxwell?"

Tessa's lungs ached to expel the breath she held, but Mr. Behr's question locked it in place.

Mr. Kilgore struck a match on the bottom of his boot and lit his cigar. "Gideon Maxwell is in for a surprise. I'll let you know when I have the details worked out." He puffed on the cigar. "As soon as that mapmaker, Feldman, gets those altered land grant maps back to us, we can set our plans into motion. I just hope they'll look like the originals."

"You have nothing to fear, Mr. Kilgore. I've seen some of

Mr. Feldman's work. He is truly an artist. The people with whom I work recommended him, and they are the best at what they do."

"Good. I don't settle for anything less, and I don't allow anyone to stand in my way."

❧

Gideon nudged the gelding through a wooded area and picked his way around a patch of scrub pines. His stomach rumbled a complaint, reminding him that breakfast was long past, but he pushed on. He hoped cutting through the woods would shave a couple of hours off his journey.

The memory of last night dogged him every mile. The alarmed expression on Tessa's face kept intruding across his mind. He couldn't run from it. "I practically forced myself on her. No wonder she ran off."

The horse twitched his ears and snorted like he agreed with every word.

"Why did I do that? If some guy had taken liberties with Martha, I'd have punched him in the nose." He pulled off his hat and wiped the sweat from his face with his neckerchief.

The warbling of a meadowlark provided the background music as Tessa's image slipped easily into his thoughts again. Her face felt exactly as he thought it would—velvety soft, like the supple kidskin gloves he sold in the store. No, softer than that. That loose wisp of hair that had grazed her cheek resembled the silk threads he remembered his mother using. The radiance of the sunset behind her had given her an ethereal glow. How could he *not* lean down to kiss her?

"But she turned her head and pulled away. Why did she do that?"

As he emerged from the stretch of woods, the road lay just ahead. He nudged the chestnut gelding into a mile-eating lope.

Minutes later, as he crested a hill, a group of three men

with cumbersome-looking equipment appeared in the distance. One set a boxlike apparatus atop a tripod while the other two proceeded farther across the meadow with their gear.

"Surveyors." What were they surveying way out here?

fourteen

"She was acting so strange."

Gideon listened as Martha told him about Tessa's visit to the mercantile.

"She looked at several different ribbons but didn't buy any. When I asked her if she was looking for a particular color, she acted like she didn't even hear me. Then she left the things she'd purchased for the boardinghouse sitting on the counter and walked out the door without them. I had to run after her to give them to her."

While it wasn't unusual for Tessa to be reserved and quiet, Martha's description of her behavior weighed heavily on his heart. Was she upset by the way he'd tried to kiss her the other night?

He took a sip of his coffee and cleared his throat. "Maybe she was just distracted. She might have had a lot on her mind." He made his voice sound as nonchalant as possible, but his heart grieved.

What if she was having second thoughts about working in such close proximity to him? He'd kick himself if his impulsive action ruined everything. Maybe she just didn't feel the same way about him as he felt about her. His gut wrenched at the thought. As soon as he stopped by the livery to see Cully, he'd make a visit to the boardinghouse.

Martha refilled his coffee cup. "Ted's mother and I plan to work on my wedding dress today, unless you need me here."

Gideon ran his finger around the rim of his cup. "I have two errands to run this morning, so if you could mind the store for about an hour, I'd appreciate it."

He descended the stairs and slipped out the back door of the storeroom. The cornflower blue sky promised a beautiful day. He hoped it would be in more ways than just the weather.

❧

Gideon walked around the boardinghouse to the backyard where Miss Pearl was hanging freshly washed sheets on the clothesline. "Morning, Miss Pearl."

The woman smiled through the clothespins held in her teeth. She removed the wooden pins and hugged Gideon. "You're back a day early. Did you get the stove parts?"

He grinned. "Sure did. I stopped at the livery and told Cully. He said he'd have them hooked up by this afternoon."

"Oh, that's just fine. But I don't suppose you came here to pass the time with an old lady like me." She gave him a sly smile. "Tessa's in the kitchen."

"You're beautiful, Miss Pearl, even with clothespins sticking out of your mouth."

She flapped her hand in his direction. "Oh, mercy sakes! Go on with you." She returned to her task, humming a tuneless ditty.

He took the porch steps two at a time and rapped lightly on the back door. When Tessa opened the door, he pulled his hat off and drew in a shallow breath.

She was a vision, even with strands of her sandy hair refusing to stay within the confines of their pins. Her cheeks were flushed a becoming shade of pink, but apprehension filled her eyes.

"Good morning, Gideon." She stepped aside so he could enter, then filled a coffee cup and set it on the table for him.

He took that as a good sign. At least she was willing for him to stay as long as it would take him to drink the coffee. "Morning." He lowered himself to the chair and watched her at the stove.

Her green-checked apron enhanced her hazel eyes as she placed a plate of fragrant cinnamon rolls on the table.

"Mm, thanks. Those smell great."

Silence hung between them as words eluded him.

Tessa appeared nervous, like she had something on her mind but didn't know how to begin. "Gideon, I have to tell—"

"Tessa, I need to—"

They exchanged uncomfortable smiles.

"There's something I heard—"

"Tessa, about the other night—"

Tessa twisted her fingers then gestured in his direction. "You go ahead."

Perhaps if he let her air out her feelings, he might be able to better address them. "No, please. You first."

She turned her back and picked up the corner of her apron. "There's something I need to tell you, but I'm afraid when I do you'll think ill of me."

The memory of the last time he jumped to conclusions stirred in his stomach. "Tessa, I won't think badly of you. I realize I did once, and I'm so very sorry I misjudged you."

She turned slowly to face him, the hem of her apron tangled around her fingers. "I didn't mean to eavesdrop, really. I was cleaning off tables in the dining room, and Mr. Kilgore left his office door open. He was talking so loud. . .I couldn't help hearing him. And then yesterday, when I saw him coming toward me on the boardwalk, I just didn't want to have an encounter with him, so I stepped into the alley behind some crates. I didn't know he would stop to talk with Mr. Behr right beside the alley."

Gideon reached over and pulled out the other chair at the table, inviting her to be seated. "Tessa, slow down. You're not making sense. Take a deep breath, and come sit down."

She gingerly slid down onto the chair, her eyes downcast. "I know it's wrong to eavesdrop. I didn't do it on purpose."

She raised her eyes to meet his. "I don't want you to think I'm the kind of person who listens at doors or snoops around trying to overhear things not meant for me."

Gideon's lips twitched. It simply wasn't conceivable for Tessa to do anything sinister. She was too unassuming. "Tessa, nobody is accusing you of doing any such thing."

"But Gideon, I heard something by accident that you need to know about. I've struggled trying to decide whether or not to tell you. It feels like repeating gossip. But it's not gossip. Mr. Kilgore is planning something that isn't right, and I'm afraid it can hurt you."

"Hurt me?" Gideon frowned.

Anything Kilgore did wouldn't surprise him, but he was more concerned with Tessa at the moment. His attempt to kiss her didn't seem to be bothering her, but whatever she'd overheard upset her to the point she was even now mangling the edge of her apron.

"Tessa, it's all right. Whatever you heard wasn't your fault. It doesn't sound as if you set out to eavesdrop on purpose. But if Kilgore has something up his sleeve that you feel I should know, I'm listening."

She gave him a hint of a wobbly smile, and his heart rolled over. If relief was a tangible thing, it spilled over her countenance like handfuls of cold water.

He could clearly see she'd been worried about his reaction. To put her at ease, he broke a cinnamon roll in two and slid one half over to her. "Come on. Share this delicacy with me, and tell me what's on your mind."

Fifteen minutes later, Gideon tried to make sense of everything Tessa had disclosed. His impression of Hubert Behr was that of a fine, upstanding, Christian gentleman. But if that was the case, what dealings did he have with Kilgore? "Did they say anything else? I don't understand what he means by altered land grant maps."

Tessa shook her head. "I don't either. He said you were in for a surprise, and his voice sounded so hateful when he said it. Do you think you should speak with the town sheriff?"

Everything Tessa had told him pinched his eyebrows into a V. "No, Sheriff McCoy is one of Kilgore's puppets. I doubt he'd do anything to help if he's in Kilgore's back pocket." He rubbed his chin. "If I telegraphed the U.S. marshal, he isn't going to come all the way out here based on our suspicions."

Tessa set her elbow on the table and leaned her chin into her hand. "So what should we do?"

Gideon's heart did a little flip at her question, and he decided to tuck away the "we" for future consideration. "First thing we're going to do is pray about it. After that. . .well, I've made a mess of things too many times running ahead of God."

Tessa looked at him squarely in the eye, like she was weighing his answer. A hint of a smile tilted the corner of her mouth. "Prayer is a good start. I'll certainly be praying."

Gideon ignored the heat rising from his middle. "I. . .uh. . . I sort of thought, well, maybe we could. . .pray together."

Tessa's eyes widened, and she raised her chin off her palm. "Together?"

His breath constricted in his throat. If she had any discomfort or misgivings about spending time in close proximity with him, she would express it now.

She clasped her hands and dropped her gaze to study her fingers. At least she was no longer mutilating the hem of her apron.

He waited.

Finally she spoke. "Gideon. . ." Her voice was as soft as an angel's song. "Your invitation is very kind, but I think I'd best pray alone."

Gideon's shoulders slumped. She was, no doubt, trying to distance herself from him. A wave of self-condemnation crashed over him, but he pushed his disappointment away lest it color the tone of his voice. "That's all right." He filled his lungs slowly, deliberately then released the air. "Tessa, about the other night. . . I apologize if I frightened you or if my behavior was ungentlemanly."

He saw her stiffen, but she didn't raise her eyes.

"Forgive me?"

The tiny shake of her head was so slight he almost missed it. No? She didn't forgive him?

She lowered her hands to her lap and began worrying the corner of her apron again.

Indecision gnawed at him. Should he excuse himself and leave? Should he wait to see if she had anything else to say?

Just as he sought God's advice, Tessa cleared her throat. "Gideon, you've never been anything but a gentleman. There's nothing to forgive."

If his heart could have burst free of his rib cage and taken wing, he'd have cheered it on. A fleeting thought sprinted through his head. Should he make another attempt to kiss her? Maybe not. Not yet, anyway.

She rose from the table, and he followed suit. "I stopped by the livery this morning and told Cully the stove parts are here. He said he could install them this afternoon, so your stove will be ready later today."

Anticipation filled her expression. "That's nice. Very nice." The corner of her apron hung twisted like a little girl's ringlet.

"We can hang your sign up in the window this afternoon if you'd like."

A nervous smile wobbled across her face. "I'd like that very much."

He stepped toward the door, but her voice lassoed him. "Gideon?"

He turned.

"I've never prayed *with* anyone before. Except Mama. I'm

afraid I might not do it right."

A slow smile worked its way up from deep within his chest and spread to his face. "Tessa, there's no wrong way to pray. God just loves hearing from His children. Besides, if our prayers had to line up with a list of rules, I've been doing it wrong for years."

Tessa's laugh fell on his ears like music, and she nodded. "Okay then. Maybe praying together would be all right." She lifted her fingers in a half wave as he headed toward the door. "I'll see you this afternoon."

He almost tripped over the threshold going out the door.

❮

Tessa dumped bread dough on the floured table and sank her fists into the soft, elastic blob. Methodically she pushed the air bubbles out of the mass, folded it over, and rolled her knuckles through it again and again, until the dough was satiny smooth. After dividing it into four equal parts, she greased the pans with lard and laid a portion of dough in each one.

Miss Pearl came in the kitchen toting her empty laundry basket on one hip. "I can't tell you how wonderful it is having you here doing the baking." The woman gave a pleasant sigh and dropped the basket by the door. "It's kind of nice having a friend in the kitchen, too. Coffee?" She withdrew two cups from the shelf.

"I just made a fresh pot." Tessa placed the pans of bread to rise at the back of the stove where warmth still lingered from breakfast. "There are a couple of cinnamon rolls left."

"You're going to spoil me for sure." Miss Pearl filled the two cups. "I don't suppose watching my figure is an excuse not to indulge." She bit into a roll and closed her eyes. "Mmm."

Tessa smiled at her landlady and took the seat opposite her. "I can check the laundry on the line for you and bring it in when it's dry."

"That would be a big help. I'm doing all the bedding today. It's a big job."

The steam from Tessa's cup sent fragrant tendrils wafting by her nose, coaxing her to take a sip. The coffee's bracing flavor lent her a bit of courage. "Miss Pearl, do you ever wish you had someone to talk to—someone special, someone you loved?"

Miss Pearl gave her a knowing look. "Missing your mama, are you?"

Tessa nodded wordlessly.

The woman took another slow sip of her coffee and set her cup down in front of her. "I'm not your mama, but if you've got something troubling on your mind, I'm a good listener."

Tessa bit her lip to command the stinging behind her eyelids to quit. She swallowed hard, forcing her emotions into line. Her eyes locked onto the dark liquid in her cup, and she willed her thoughts to fall into the right order so they wouldn't sound stupid. "Miss Pearl, did anyone ever try to kiss you?"

A snuffled sound came from Miss Pearl's side of the table. When Tessa looked up, the woman's eyes twinkled, her lips pressed together, and the corners of her mouth appeared to have the hiccups.

Miss Pearl cleared her throat and finally spoke. Her voice reminded Tessa of a tinkling music box. "Well, yes. I remember the first time my Jacob tried to kiss me. We were standing behind an old willow tree where he'd carved our initials. He leaned way over, his eyes all squinched closed and his lips pooched out like a guppy."

Tessa tried to paint the picture in her mind, and a smile tugged at her lips. "What happened?"

"Teacher rang the bell. Recess was over."

A laugh bubbled up from Tessa's middle, releasing the tightness in her chest. "How old were you?"

A faraway look crept into Miss Pearl's eyes. "He was eleven, and I was nine. But I knew from that moment he was the man I would marry."

"And did you?"

"Mm-hmm."

Tessa could see memory's pages turning backward in the woman's mind. "I was just sixteen. We married and worked side by side together for twenty-six years. Fever took Jacob twelve years ago." She smiled at Tessa. "Sometimes I can still taste that first kiss."

A flutter tickled Tessa's stomach, and she drew in a soft breath. How sweet would it be to hide a memory that special in one's heart?

"So"—Miss Pearl picked up her cup again and eyed Tessa over its rim—"may I assume Gideon kissed you?"

"No." She blurted out the reply as a rush of heat filled her face and burned her ears. She gentled her voice. "No—that is, he started to, but. . . ."

"But what? Teacher didn't ring the bell."

Tessa blew out a stiff sigh. "I pulled away from him. And I don't know why."

Miss Pearl's smile crinkled the lines around her eyes. "Maybe you just weren't ready, child. A girl wants to know a man cares about her here." She laid a hand over her heart. "And she has to know how she feels about him, too. Do you know how you feel about Gideon?"

Tessa lifted her shoulders slightly. "I–I'm not sure."

"Well, there's one way to find out for sure." The woman reached across the table and patted Tessa's hand. "You talk to God about it. He'll reveal those feelings to you, so you don't have to wonder if it's right or not."

Tessa returned Miss Pearl's smile. "Seems like I have a lot to pray about."

"You take it to the Father. You can trust Him, honey girl."

Honey girl. She never thought she'd hear those words again. The sweet endearment wrapped around her heart like a warm quilt. The grief she felt at missing her mama suddenly wasn't quite so sharp.

fifteen

The reproach on Tessa's face took Gideon aback.

"Don't you like horses?"

Tessa's shoulders hunched with a slight shake of her head. "It's not that... It's really none of my business."

Gideon laid aside the letter from the breeder in Illinois he'd shown her moments ago. Judging by her frown, she didn't share his enthusiasm. Maybe her stony silence was because she feared she'd no longer have the bakery. "Hey, don't be concerned about the buyer not wanting to keep the bakery. Business has doubled in the past couple of weeks because you're here."

She fingered the wiggly ridges around the edge of a pie for several long moments. Not meeting his eyes, she pursed her lips before answering. "My father had a good farm in Indiana—at least it could have been a good farm if he'd worked at it. But he sold it and dragged Mama and me out here to chase an illusive dream of getting rich. Mama had been sickly for so long, and traveling was too hard on her. She might still be alive today if we'd stayed put. I don't understand how a man can throw away a perfectly good means of support for his family in favor of such an uncertain prospect."

An invisible fist punched Gideon in the gut. He swallowed the ire rising in his chest only to feel disappointment replace it. For weeks he'd wondered and prayed about Tessa possibly being the woman God had chosen for him. But her disdain of his dream was a bucket of cold water thrown in his face. How could she compare his plans to her father's drunken irresponsibility?

"Tessa, this is something I've planned for a long time. I'm not entering into this with my eyes shut." He wished she'd look at him. "There's a huge need in this area for sturdy, well-bred farm horses."

She cocked her head to one side. "But you told me your father started this business and that he supported his family well because of the dependable reputation he built as a merchant. Why would you cast that aside on a gamble?"

Defensiveness sprang up and grabbed control of his words before he could stop it. "I'm not casting anything aside, and I'm certainly not gambling away my father's hard work. Being a merchant suited him. He enjoyed the work. I just want something different." He didn't add that he'd hoped for her support of his dream. He'd sought God's guidance in this endeavor for three years and felt assured of the Lord's approval. But for weeks Tessa's image had begun entering into that dream as well, and it was an image he didn't want to dismiss.

"Mmm. Something sure smells good in here." Ty Sawyer strolled in the door. "What's this? You operatin' a bakery now?"

Gideon shoved his disconcertment down and greeted his friend. "Hey, Ty."

Ty stopped short, and his eyes widened at the sight of Tessa in her green gingham apron. He yanked his hat from his head. "Don't believe I've had the pleasure."

The silly grin on his friend's face caused Gideon to grit his teeth, but courtesy demanded he at least make the introduction. "Tessa Langford, Ty Sawyer."

Ty swept his hand across his middle and executed a courtly bow. "Miss Tessa, pleased to meet you."

Gideon stifled a growl. "What brings you to town again so soon, Ty?"

Ty leaned against the counter. "I came in to make my loan payment at the bank. But I saw something while I was standing there waiting that I thought you'd be real interested in."

"What's that?"

Ty took off his neckerchief and wiped the sweatband of his hat. "I'd just stepped up to the window when the clerk asked me to wait for a minute and went into Sewell's office with a handful of papers. He left the door open, and I could see Kilgore and Behr sittin' in there with Sewell." Ty paused like he was waiting for Gideon's reaction. "I'd give a week's wages to know what was going on in there, wouldn't you?"

Gideon rubbed his chin. "Kilgore and Behr—both in there with Mr. Sewell?"

"Mm-hmm."

"Were they're doing anything illegal?"

Ty stuck his hand into the gumdrop jar. "What do you think?"

"I think I have work to do, and I think you owe me about twenty-five cents now for all the gumdrops you've eaten in the past month." He lifted a crate of sewing notions to the counter and pried off the top.

"Look, Gideon, if this guy Behr is doing business with Kilgore, you better watch your back."

A frown forced Gideon's brows downward. "I appreciate you telling me about this, Ty, but what can I do? Even if I thought they were doing something illegal, the sheriff isn't going to do anything since he answers to Kilgore."

"Gideon?"

He'd almost forgotten Tessa was standing there. The stricken look on her face indicated she'd all but forgotten their earlier disagreement.

"Gideon, I feel terrible. I should have told you sooner about what I overheard."

He took a step closer to her, deliberately moving between her and Ty. "Tessa, we don't even know what they're up to yet. It could be something completely legitimate."

"Pfft." Ty grunted. "You really believe that?"

Gideon shrugged. "Truthfully, no. But until we can prove otherwise, all we can do is wait and see."

Ty shrugged. "Suppose you're right." He turned and bestowed a huge smile on Tessa. "Miss Tessa, there's gonna be a barn dance next Saturday night over at the Johnson place. I'd be pleased to escort you."

Gideon's insides twisted. He sucked in a breath and shot daggers at the guy who was supposed to be his best friend. But Ty seemed oblivious, standing there twisting his hat, waiting for Tessa's reply.

No, Tessa. Tell him no.

Tessa's lashes dropped to her cheeks in a demure pose as a tiny smile curved her lips. "Why, Mr. Sawyer, that's so kind of you to ask."

If one could chew his own teeth, Gideon gave it his best effort.

A ridiculous-sounding chuckle came from Ty's direction, and Gideon suppressed the urge to throw the jar of gumdrops at him. *As soon as Ty leaves, I'm going to ask you myself, Tessa, so just tell him no.*

She gave Ty a sweet smile. "Martha was telling me about the barn dance just yesterday. I'm sorry, but I've already made plans to attend with someone else."

Ty's grin drooped, and he shuffled his feet for a moment. "Oh. Well, maybe I'll see you there." He plopped his hat back on his head and lifted a hand in good-bye.

Gideon barely acknowledged Ty's leaving. Instead his eyes followed Tessa as she turned toward the storeroom. Who had already asked her to the barn dance? "Tessa?"

Tessa turned in the doorway. "Yes?"

"Um, about the barn dance. . ."

"Gideon, if you don't mind, could we talk later? I need to get these pies in the oven, and the heat is just right."

His head bounced up and down. "Oh, sure. You go right ahead. Don't let me keep you."

❧

The courage to inquire about the man with whom Tessa planned to attend the barn dance eluded Gideon for days. He'd managed to initiate topics about almost everything else, but he couldn't bring himself to speculate on the identity of the man who would hold Tessa in his arms and waltz her across the barn floor. Perhaps it didn't matter, since Tessa's opinion of his dream still left a bitter taste in his mouth.

The bell on the door jingled.

Gideon looked up to greet his customer, but the words stuck in his throat. He'd mulled over the information Ty gave him several days ago, as well as the conversation Tessa had overheard, but came to no conclusions.

Now Hubert Behr entered the store wearing the same dignified expression he'd worn the first day Gideon met him. "A pleasant afternoon to you, young fellow. Might I have a word with you?"

Warning signals shot through Gideon's head. "Good afternoon, Mr. Behr. How may I help you today?"

Behr cleared his throat. "First off, I must apologize for the delay in getting back to you. My business here has taken a bit longer than I expected. I do hope the mercantile is still available for purchase."

Gideon glanced in Tessa's direction and saw a frown flit across her face at the mention of selling the mercantile. With Ty's information in mind, Gideon exercised caution before replying. "I thought you might leave Willow Creek as soon as your business was finished."

One thick eyebrow lifted slightly as Behr silently questioned Gideon's response. "No, I'm not planning to leave anytime soon. I would like to make an offer on your place, but it will take at least a couple of weeks before I can finalize any plans."

The man named a figure that matched Gideon's original asking price.

Gideon studied Behr's face, searching for signs of deceit or corruption. "Sir, if I might be so bold, may I speak frankly?"

Behr nodded. "Of course, young man. What's on your mind?"

The store was empty at the moment, but the presence of Tessa's Bakery had increased the number of customers coming and going, and Gideon didn't want to be interrupted. He spoke quietly and quickly. "Mr. Behr, you seemed like a decent sort when you first arrived. But I must say I've been more than a bit concerned to see you in the company of Henry Kilgore numerous times. I apologize if I'm out of line, but I feel I should warn you. You would do well to be careful in dealing with Mr. Kilgore."

Hubert Behr's gray eyes narrowed and scrutinized Gideon for a long minute. Just when Gideon was certain he'd not only overstepped his bounds but probably also ruined any chance of selling the mercantile, Behr finally spoke. "Young man, you seem to know more than you are letting on; so let me caution *you*. Employ discretion before proceeding."

Gideon glanced in the direction of the storeroom where he could hear Tessa humming as she worked. He wanted no confrontation with Hubert Behr with Tessa close by.

He took a deep breath and met Behr's steady gaze. "Sir, I have reason to believe you are engaged in business with Henry Kilgore. He's probably told you by now that I've refused to sell him the mercantile."

Behr showed no reaction.

"My decision not to sell to Kilgore is based on several reasons, both personal and ethical."

The front door opened, and two ladies entered carrying large market baskets over their arms.

Gideon threw Behr a pointed look before greeting his

customers. "Morning, ladies. How may I help you?"

The women both declared they wished to purchase baked goods, and while Tessa filled their orders, they browsed through the bolts of cloth, exclaiming at the colors and choices.

Gideon motioned to Behr to step over nearer the door to put more space between them and the ladies. "Mr. Behr, I'm sorry, but I can only assume you're here as a proxy for Kilgore, trying to purchase the mercantile for him."

Behr lowered his head and slipped his hand inside his jacket pocket.

Gideon nailed an unblinking stare at Behr's arm, waiting to see if the man might pull out a derringer. His mind raced along with his pulse making lightning decisions how to position himself to protect Tessa and his customers.

Through the thick curtain of tension, one of the ladies called to him. "Mr. Maxwell, might I get a dress length of this cloth, please? And I'll need some thread and buttons as well."

Gideon didn't take his eyes off Behr as he replied in a voice he hoped sounded natural. "Of course, Mrs. Clary. I'll be right there." He paused to see if Behr would react. When he didn't, Gideon excused himself and went to meet his customer's need, hoping Behr would simply leave. He started to measure out the yardage the woman requested when he heard Tessa's voice.

"Would you care to sample some of these cinnamon cookies or perhaps some pound cake, sir?"

Gideon's eyes widened as Behr crossed to stand next to Tessa and accept a tidbit from her tray.

All spit evaporated from his mouth, and clumsiness attacked his fingers. After managing to cut and fold the material for the woman, he hurriedly added up the other purchases and finalized the transaction. "Thank you, ladies.

Come again."

He turned to where Behr was still standing and chatting with Tessa.

She handed him a bag, and he paid her for his purchase. "I hope you enjoy it, sir."

"I'm sure I shall, young lady."

Gideon took Tessa's arm and gently pushed her toward the storeroom, positioning himself in front of her. "Mr. Behr, I doubt we have any more to say to each other, so I'll ask you to leave now."

He heard a soft gasp behind him. "Gideon!"

Behr's expression did not change, but his eyes shifted toward the door. "Mr. Maxwell, is there a place we can speak privately where we won't be interrupted? I fear I have given you the wrong impression."

Gideon folded his arms across his chest. "Mr. Behr, you've been seen in Henry Kilgore's company on numerous occasions, and you've been heard exchanging business plans with him. Earlier today you and Kilgore were meeting with Roland Sewell. Exactly what impression was I supposed to get?"

Behr glanced past Gideon's shoulder where Tessa still stood. "I can see you won't be satisfied until I reveal my true purpose for being here. If you will trust me, I'd like to meet with you anywhere you say, someplace private, so I can clear up this misunderstanding."

Gideon deepened his frown. "I have no reason to trust you, sir."

The thick mustache on Behr's lip tweaked. "Very prudent, young man. But if you will allow me, I will prove I am worthy of your trust. However, we should not be seen leaving the store together. Tell me where you'd like to meet, and I shall be there."

"Gideon. . ." Tessa's frightened whisper tugged at him.

The man's odd statement aroused deeper suspicion, but

Gideon slowly nodded. Without taking his eyes off Behr, he spoke to Tessa. "Tessa, would you mind taking care of the store for a short time? I don't think this will take long."

The silence was broken only by Tessa's sharp intake of air.

After probing Behr's face for a full minute, Gideon spoke. "Take the main street through the edge of town past the livery stable. There's a grove of cottonwoods and elm trees to your right. Beyond that, you'll see the town cemetery. Meet me by the pines on the far side of the cemetery. It's about a ten-minute walk." Gideon pulled out his pocket watch. "I'll be there by two o'clock."

Behr nodded and walked out the door.

Tessa gripped Gideon's sleeve. "Gideon, please don't go there alone. What if it's a trap? What if he brings Mr. Kilgore with him? When Mr. Kilgore said you were in for a surprise, his voice was so cold and hateful. Gideon, please don't go."

sixteen

Gideon berated himself as he approached the stand of pines at the far end of the cemetery. If Behr was luring him into a trap as Tessa feared, the spot was too remote to expect help to arrive quickly should the need arise. Indecision caused Gideon's steps to hesitate. Should he abort this meeting or see what the man had to say?

Hubert Behr stepped out of the shadows. "Thank you for coming, Mr. Maxwell."

Gideon gave the man a wary nod.

Behr reached into his coat pocket and extracted a wallet. "I should begin by telling you my real purpose for being in Willow Creek." He opened the leather folder and displayed the identification within.

Gideon studied the pewter badge and the words engraved around it, unsure whether to believe what Behr was indicating. "Pinkerton National Detective Agency. You're a Pinkerton agent?"

"I am." Mr. Behr's tone, though modulated, held the ring of authority.

Abrasive edges of puzzlement troubled Gideon. "What business would a Pinkerton have in a town the size of Willow Creek, Iowa?"

Behr tucked the wallet away. "The Chicago, Kansas and Nebraska Railroad received a most interesting letter from Mr. Roland Sewell describing some rather creative land deals Henry Kilgore was attempting to put together. Included were Mr. Kilgore's ongoing practices of intimidating business owners and landowners in this area to sell to him at deflated prices. The railroad contacted the General Land Office in Washington, which in turn contacted our Chicago office requesting that we investigate Mr. Kilgore's activities and gather tangible evidence of fraudulent transactions."

Skepticism tussled with relief in Gideon's mind. Behr seemed to use all the right words and phrases, and the identification he'd displayed moments ago bore silent testimony to the man's explanation.

Behr interlaced his hands in front of him and cleared his throat. "I might ask you how you knew I was meeting with Mr. Kilgore and Mr. Sewell earlier today, but that's not really important. However, I would like to prevail upon what I suspect is your sense of honor and request your assistance."

Gideon guarded his expression while he digested Hubert Behr's revelation of his identity. *A Pinkerton agent!* If that were truly the case, Gideon had a few questions. He steeled his eyes. "Mr. Behr, how do you explain the overheard conversations in which you indicated entering into a partnership with Kilgore?"

A slight shrug lifted Behr's shoulders. "One of the distasteful parts of this business, young man. Sometimes the investigating agent must employ a bit of fiction before the suspect will relax enough to divulge information we need to build a case. Speaking untruths is not something to which I aspire. Unfortunately, I've recently found it necessary to lead Mr. Kilgore to believe my occupation is procuring land for the railroad—with a willingness to engage in private land speculation on the side."

"And the reference to altered land grant maps?"

Behr's bushy eyebrows arched slightly, but Gideon didn't plan on naming Tessa as the one who overheard the conversations.

"The surveyors, as well as the cartographer hired by Mr. Kilgore, were taken into custody this morning without Mr.

Kilgore's knowledge. My agency is now in possession of the maps, which were rather masterfully revised, I must say. The forgeries appear to be quite authentic. They were the last piece of evidence I needed. All that remains now is to take Mr. Kilgore into custody."

Gideon weighed the credibility of the man's answer. The memory of the slight tremble in Tessa's voice accompanying her urge for caution gave him pause. Another question nagged him.

"If all this is true, how does your offer to buy the mercantile fit in? How can I be sure you aren't making a deal for Kilgore?"

Behr didn't blink. "You can't, young man. Life is full of uncertainties. That's why God's Word encourages us to learn wisdom and discretion." His eyes remained fastened on Gideon, but his mustache twitched. "Even Pinkerton agents tire of adventure after a time and desire a bit of a slower pace. My investigating days are drawing to a close. I can assure you my offer is legitimate. I've shown my identification credentials and given an explanation. I can't make you believe me."

Gideon took a slow, deep breath. "Exactly what is it you're asking me to do?"

Behr smiled. "Send word to Kilgore that you've changed your mind about selling the mercantile to him and you now wish to discuss a deal."

&

Tessa glanced toward the door for the hundredth time since Gideon left, then she looked at the clock. Had it really only been twenty minutes since he followed Mr. Behr to the agreed-upon meeting place? Anxiety weighed in her chest where she knew faith should reside.

The scriptures she'd read in the past weeks about God's care and protection echoed in her mind, along with her mother's repeated admonition that God was worthy of her trust. Such trust was a choice, much like the choice she'd made months ago to survive to honor Mama's memory.

She finished sprinkling cinnamon sugar over the top of a pan of scones and slid it into the oven. Wiping her hands on a towel, she squared her shoulders. Those days following Mama's funeral, Tessa believed her survival depended upon herself and her own perseverance. Reading the precious words in Mama's Bible and remembering the faith she'd learned at her mother's knee birthed fresh understanding of God's care. Even now she realized she could do nothing to ensure Gideon's safety, and his well-being depended completely upon God's grace. She whispered a prayer for God's protection.

Her disagreement with Gideon earlier in the week made little sense now. Admittedly Gideon's well-thought-out plan of raising farm horses in no way resembled Papa's selfish whims. Furthermore, a man didn't share his dreams and goals expecting rejection.

After several restless nights, understanding had dawned. Gideon confided his plans to her because they were friends. No, more than friends. He'd almost kissed her.

Every time she was in his presence, contentment warmed her and there was nowhere else she wanted to be. When she was apart from him, she ached with a longing that only his return satisfied. The times she caught him gazing at her or when he sent her a toe-curling smile, an entire colony of butterflies turned loose in her stomach. How could she deny the connection that existed between them?

Shame filled her when she remembered the hurtful words she'd carelessly tossed at Gideon's dream. She determined to apologize for her thoughtlessness as soon as he returned. She glanced once more at the door, hoping for a glimpse of him.

Keep busy. He'll be back in a few minutes.

Miss Pearl had requested some potato rolls to serve with her pot roast, and they were popular items in the bakery as well. *Keep busy.* She blended softened yeast into the batter, adding flour with leftover mashed potatoes until the dough became stiff. Her knuckles plunged into the dough and began the rhythmic kneading action.

"Well, well. I'd heard you and Maxwell had a cozy little arrangement here, but I wasn't sure I believed it."

Tessa spun around. Henry Kilgore stood in the storeroom doorway. She hadn't heard him come in. A shudder rippled through her. "If you want to speak to Gideon, he's not here."

Kilgore sauntered into the storeroom, casting a disdainful perusal at the results of Gideon's painstaking work. "I don't need to talk to him. You're the one I came to see. I wondered if you'd given any more thought to my offer."

Offer? What offer? Surely he didn't mean. . . . "Mr. Kilgore, I made it quite clear when I quit my job at the hotel that I had no intention of working for you in any capacity. Ever."

Kilgore's laugh lacked even a shred of humor. "Never say never, my dear. I'm certain you'll come around to my way of thinking."

Nausea swelled in her stomach, and the air she tried to drag into her lungs suddenly felt thick. "That will *never* happen. And I'm *not* your dear. You can leave now."

He took two more steps in her direction. "I can't leave yet. We've haven't had a chance to sit down for a nice talk. Why don't you come over to my place, and we can discuss a business arrangement?"

Was the man deranged? Did he honestly believe he could talk her into going anywhere with him? She backed away. Panic slid its tentacles around her throat, and her stomach threatened to retch. A chill unlike anything she'd ever known invaded her bones. "Mr. Kilgore. . ." She hardly recognized her own voice as suffocating fear restricted her air.

Another voice bullied its way into her memory. *"You ain't worth nothin'."*

The past few months, she'd begun to distance herself from Papa's assessment, even daring to reject the validity of his words. But the wicked gleam in Kilgore's eyes and the insinuation of all that his "offer" entailed brought the ugliness of her father's ridicule crashing over her again.

She took another step backward and bumped into the corner that formed where the worktable met the wall shelves.

Kilgore closed the space between them, his scrutinizing gaze lingering on her in a most ungentlemanly way. Was this what Papa meant? Kilgore reached out and ran his fingers down one side of her face. When she jerked away from him, he seized her jaw in a cruel grip. "I'm a patient man, but I do have my limits. You've been in this town long enough now to know that I get what I want." He released his hold and patted her cheek.

The prayer she'd sent heavenward for Gideon's safety crossed her lips once more, only this time the petition was for herself. "I told you, Mr. Kilgore. I will not work in your saloon. Now please leave. Customers will be walking in here any minute."

"No they won't. I hung the Closed sign on the door when I came in." A slow, sinister smile slithered across Kilgore's face, and he stepped back. "You know what I heard? Gideon Maxwell isn't the choirboy you think he is. In fact, the good people of Willow Creek might be interested to know that Maxwell is a regular over at the Blue Goose."

If Kilgore's presence hadn't initiated such revulsion, she might have laughed at the insinuation. The very idea was preposterous. Did he think she would agree to go along with his proposition because he tried to make her believe Gideon visited his saloon? "That's a lie! Gideon would never go there."

Kilgore sucked on his teeth. "Maybe not, but people love a

spicy story. What do you think that will do to his credibility as an honest businessman, hmm?" A smug upturn at the corner of his mouth punctuated his question.

Tears burned her eyes, and she felt sick to her stomach. "Please don't do that to Gideon. What has he ever done to hurt you?"

All semblance of the smile faded from Kilgore's face. "He thinks he's better than me. Gideon Maxwell looks down his nose at me, just like his old man did. Holier-than-thou hypocrites, both of them. Just like the good people of the town where I grew up." A vein bulged on the side of his neck, and his chest rose and fell like the bellows in Cully's blacksmith forge. "Just because my old man was no good, all the important people in town—those fine, upstanding people who always acted like they were better than everyone else— said I had his bad blood." A grotesque sneer disfigured his face. "Gideon Maxwell is just like them. Well, I aim to teach him that nobody toys with Henry Kilgore. I will destroy Gideon Maxwell. Unless. . ."

Fear rose up to strangle her once more. Even without Kilgore finishing his thought, she knew what his conditions were. He moved close to her again and wrapped his fingers around a handful of her hair. She couldn't draw enough air to scream.

He leaned in so close she felt his hot breath on her face. "You come with me now, or I promise you, before the day is out, I'll see to it that Gideon Maxwell's good name and reputation are so sullied he'll lose the respect of everyone in this town. People will spit on him just like they used to do to me. But no more."

If Kilgore did what he threatened, the dream Gideon had shared with her a few days before would shatter at his feet. She couldn't let that happen.

Kilgore grabbed her arm and pulled her toward the back

door. "You keep your mouth shut when we step out, or so help me, you'll wish you had."

He pushed her out the door in front of him, and when he did so, the gingham apron she wore—Mama's apron—caught on the hook Gideon used to latch the door at night. A ripping sound reached her ears. When she tried to rescue the garment, Kilgore clamped his fingers around her upper arm and twisted her flesh. She bit her lip to keep from crying out.

"You won't be needing that apron anymore." Kilgore's hateful gloat seared her heart. Papa's jeering words echoed in her head again, mocking the effort she'd made in the past months to live in a way to make her mother proud.

He dragged her along beside him as they stepped out from behind the telegraph office on their way across the street to the Blue Goose. When they entered the establishment, the odor of whiskey and smoke assaulted her senses. Jeering catcalls from the men leaning against the bar and indecent invitations from others seated at the tables brought tears to her eyes. A hand reached out and pinched her as they passed. It was her nightmare come to life.

God, protect me.

"Hands off, boys. She's off-limits." Kilgore tugged her up against him, out of the reach of the groping hands. A maniacal grin spread his lips. "At least for now."

One man wearing a dirty, sweat-stained shirt with missing buttons bellowed, "Ain't our money good enough for her?"

Kilgore forced her through a doorway at the back of the smoke-filled room. "In due time, gentlemen. For now, she's mine."

He pulled the door shut behind them and pushed her down a narrow hallway. Muffled voices and laughter came from behind a row of closed doors.

God, please help me.

When they reached the last door, Kilgore pulled a key

from his pocket and inserted it in the lock. Thrusting the door open, he shoved her into what she assumed was his private room.

Heavy draperies hung at the window, blocking out most of the light. Whiskey bottles and glasses sat on a small table. A wooden chair took up one corner. Maroon velvet covered the bed positioned in the opposite corner.

He locked the door behind him. "Now then, you and I need to get to know one another. Sit down there." He indicated the chair.

Heavenly Father, don't let this man touch me. "Mr. Kilgore, please don't do this."

"I thought we had a deal," he hissed, raking his gaze over her in a way that made her feel like the deed he insinuated had already been done. "Not that it matters now."

Through her paralyzing fear, words she'd heard over and over in her dreams came back to whisper in her ear once again.

"Tessa, God says you are precious in His sight, and I agree with Him."

seventeen

Gideon cut through the alley behind the telegraph office mulling over Hubert Behr's words. As he approached the back door of the store, his steps slowed.

The door stood open, and smoke drifted out.

He closed the distance in a few long strides and leaped up the steps. A blue gray cloud filled the bakery area. Had she gotten distracted by customers out front? "Tessa?"

He jogged through the storeroom and past the store counter. Odd. Why was the front door shut and the CLOSED sign displayed?

"Tessa!" A sweeping glance told him she was nowhere in the store.

He strode back to Tessa's work area and yanked the oven door open. Smoke billowed from blackened lumps inside. Tessa wouldn't leave something in the oven like this, unless. . . *"Tessa!"*

Where could she have gone? He turned to head out the back door when a small green-checked scrap of cloth on the latch caught his eye. Tessa's green gingham apron. He shoved the shredded cloth into his pocket.

His heart in his throat, he lunged out the door and raced in the direction of the boardinghouse. There was no sign of her along the boardwalk. He catapulted over the picket fence surrounding Miss Pearl's backyard and bounded up the back steps. "Miss Pearl!" He hammered on the door, gulping air.

Scurrying footsteps approached from inside, and the door flung open. "Mercy sakes, Gideon. What's wrong?"

He pushed back his panic and wiped his sleeve across his

forehead. "Is Tessa here?"

"Why, no. She likely won't be home until later this afternoon. Why?"

Without taking the time for an explanation, he bolted across the yard and hollered over his shoulder. "If she shows up, keep her here."

His pounding heart reverberated in his ears as he ran down the boardwalk, checking stores and offices as he went. The ache in his chest had nothing to do with his heaving lungs. Where could she be?

Maybe she'd gone to the hotel to see Tillie and Flossie. He dashed down the alley to the side door that opened into the hotel kitchen. Trying to keep his wits about him, he yanked it open.

The two women sent startled stares in his direction.

"Have either of you seen Tessa today?"

Tillie shook her head. "Not today. She stopped by yesterday to bring me and Flossie some—"

Gideon pushed away from the door and ran to the front door of the hotel, nearly plowing over two people who were exiting. He mumbled an apology and strode directly to the front desk. "Do you know if Mr. Behr has come in, in the last few minutes?"

The clerk behind the desk tossed Gideon a look of surprise. "Why, no. I've been here for the past several hours. If anyone had come in, I'd have known it."

Gideon lit out across the street, dodging passersby. Willow Creek's sheriff might be Kilgore's puppet, but if Gideon couldn't locate the Pinkerton agent, he was running out of choices. He found Sheriff McCoy leaned back in his chair with his feet on the desk and his hands interlaced over his chest, eyes closed.

"Sheriff!"

The man flung his arms out like he was about to take

flight. He scowled at the interruption of his nap. "What is it, Maxwell?"

"The young woman who works in my store, Tessa Langford—she's missing."

The sheriff yawned and tipped forward in his chair, bringing the two front legs down on the floor with a thump. "How long has she been missing?"

Gideon frowned with frustration. "I don't know, maybe an hour?"

Sheriff McCoy snorted. "An hour? She's probably running an errand, or out galivantin', or maybe she's got herself a beau and it ain't you. Is that what's got you so riled up?"

Gideon resisted the urge to grab the man by his shirt. Instead he turned on his heel toward the door. "I'd appreciate your help, Sheriff, if you don't have anything better to do. Miss Langford wouldn't have just up and left while she was working." He stopped in the doorway to toss a hard look at the lawman. "Isn't that what you get paid for? Or does Henry Kilgore pay you more than the town does?"

Gideon didn't wait for a reply. He stepped out onto the boardwalk ticking off a mental list of places Tessa could have gone. If she'd visited her mother's grave, he'd have seen her when he met with Behr. He'd checked all the likely places.

What if she didn't go anyplace on her own? What if she was *taken*? He stood panting on the boardwalk for a moment, his stomach in a knot. Could her father have returned? Would he have forced her to go with him?

He'd need a horse to widen his search. Cully would help him.

As he ran past the hotel, he nearly collided with Hubert Behr coming out the ornate doors.

The Pinkerton agent grabbed his sleeve. "What's going on, Maxwell? The desk clerk just told me you were looking for me."

"Tessa's missing. After I met with you, I went back to the store, and she was gone. She had something in the oven, and it was burning, and I found this." He pulled the small green-checked scrap of cloth from his pocket. "Her apron was snagged on the back door latch. Wherever she went, I don't think she wanted to go."

Behr's thick eyebrows lifted. "You think someone took her against her will?"

Gideon lifted his shoulders. "I'm beginning to think so."

Behr scanned a practiced eye down one side of the street and up the other. "Where are you going now?"

"I've looked all over town. I thought I'd get a horse from Cully and start searching out past town."

The investigator pulled his face into a frown. "You haven't sent the message to Kilgore yet, have you?"

"No." Annoyance niggled at Gideon. How could the man think about Kilgore at a time like this?

Behr nodded. "Good. Have you notified the sheriff?"

Gideon pulled his lips into a grim line. "Hmph, for all the good it will do. He's about useless."

The Pinkerton's expression indicated he understood. "All right. I'm going to comb the town, every building, every house, every place of business, every alley." He pulled out his pocket watch. "It's almost three thirty. If we haven't found her by four thirty, I'll force the sheriff to organize a search party." Behr clapped Gideon on the shoulder and set off at a brisk pace.

Gideon continued toward Cully's place, grateful for the agent's help. What direction should he look, once he was mounted? Dozens of wagon tracks led in and out of town.

He prayed as he ran down the street. *God, please protect her. Where is she, Father? Show me where she is.*

He rounded the corner and had to stop short to avoid running into two men lounging against the building, sharing a bottle.

"Didja see that pretty little new girl at the Blue Goose?"

"Sure, I saw her, but Kilgore told everybody she was off-limits. Don't see why our money ain't good enough."

Gideon's blood ran cold. He grabbed one of the men by the shoulders. "What girl?"

The man scowled. "Hey, take your hands off me."

His friend laughed. "He just wants a date with that new girl, like the rest of us. Well, you're gonna hafta get in line, buddy. There's other gals at the Blue Goose."

The two guffawed as Gideon released his grip.

The Blue Goose! Looking there hadn't even entered his mind.

He sprinted across the street and pushed the swinging doors open. A sweeping scan from one side of the room to the other didn't reveal Tessa. He strode to the bar.

A heavyset man wearing an apron polished a glass and set it in front of him. "What'll it be, friend? Whiskey?"

Gideon brushed the glass aside. "I'm looking for a girl. She might have come in here earlier—maybe with Henry Kilgore."

The bartender smirked. "You ain't the only one who'd like to get to know her better. But Mr. Kilgore's orders are—"

Gideon lunged across the bar and grabbed the man's shirtfront. "Where can I find Kilgore?"

The man's eyes darted back and forth. "He's back there in his private room. I can't disturb him now."

"Well, I can. Which room is his? Tell me now, or I'll break down every door in the place."

A sneer slid across the bartender's lips, and he released a nervous cough. "Long as you don't tell him who told you, it's the last door on the left." He jerked his thumb toward an open door that revealed a hallway.

Praying he wasn't too late, Gideon shoved his way in the direction the bartender indicated. Ignoring all the other doors, he barged toward the last one. Without bothering to knock, he tried the doorknob. Locked.

"*Tessa!*"

Thumping and crashing noises, punctuated by a terror-filled scream, filtered through the door.

Gideon took a step backward and raised his boot, ramming it with all his weight against the door. The door frame splintered and gave way.

The few pieces of furniture in the room were in disarray, broken chair pieces littered the floor. The shattered remains of a whiskey bottle lay strewed across the room.

Tessa stood in the corner, eyes wide with fear, tears streaming but unrelenting tenacity carved into her face. She gripped a broken chair leg like a formidable weapon.

Henry Kilgore leaned against the wall opposite her with his hands raised in surrender and blood trickling from his lip as well as a gash on the side of his head. "Get her out of here! She's crazy!"

Gideon plunged across the room and locked his hands around Kilgore's throat.

"*Gideon, no!* I'm all right. He didn't touch me."

Gideon threw Kilgore to the floor, his chest heaving with controlled rage and his fists clenched. He glanced up at Tessa and then to the busted door.

Hubert Behr stood in the doorway with the bartender just past his shoulder. The Pinkerton agent reached into his back pocket and extracted a pair of handcuffs. "I'll take over now, young man." He pulled Kilgore's hands around to his back and secured them.

Gideon climbed over the debris in the room and gathered Tessa into his arms. He held her trembling form tightly against his chest as she dropped the chair leg and her torrent of tears released. The fury drained from him. He tightened his arms around her and whispered against her hair, "Shh, it's all right."

Behr hauled Kilgore to his feet with surprising ease. "Allow me to reintroduce myself, sir. Hubert Behr, Pinkerton National Detective Agency, at your service. Looks like we can add kidnapping to your list of charges."

Kilgore's face registered first shock, followed by venom. "You can't do this," he spat. "She came here on her own accord."

Behr glanced at Tessa weeping in Gideon's arms. "Judging by the lady's reaction, the validity of that statement is in question. But not to worry, the charges of land fraud, falsifying official documents, and forgery will all stick." He sent Gideon a smile. "Since I plan to deliver Mr. Kilgore to the U.S. marshal myself rather than relying on your sheriff, it might take a few days before we can discuss the purchase of the mercantile."

Kilgore glared at Behr over his shoulder. "*You're* buying Maxwell's place?"

Behr prodded Kilgore toward the door.

Gideon smiled and pulled his shirttail out to wipe Tessa's tears. "Come on. Let's get you home."

ஐ

Tessa wasn't sure her shaky legs would carry her all the way to the boardinghouse, but Gideon's comforting arm around her waist steadied her. He settled her onto a kitchen chair, concern knitting his eyebrows.

As she sipped a glass of cool water, she listened as Gideon filled Miss Pearl in on the events of the afternoon. She closed her eyes, grateful that Gideon relieved her of having to speak of those horrible moments.

Miss Pearl hovered over Tessa and bustled about the kitchen in turn. "Mercy sakes, Gideon. It's a pure blessing that you got there when you did. I shudder to think what might have happened." She pushed the coffeepot onto the hot part of the stove and set a pitcher of cream and the sugar bowl on the table, clucking her tongue.

"Actually, Miss Pearl, Tessa had the situation under control before I busted down that door." He reached across the table and gave Tessa's fingers a squeeze as his dark eyes locked onto hers. "You're quite a lady, Tessa."

A burning ache crept up her throat. She dropped her gaze to her hands, unable to look at Gideon any longer. How could he say such a thing? Papa always said she was worthless, unfit for polite company. Shame filled her at the thought of Gideon having to rescue her from the tawdry back rooms of the Blue Goose.

As if reading her mind, Gideon gave her hand a gentle tug. "Tessa, you are precious in God's eyes. You know it, too. You fought for yourself. You refused to knuckle under to Kilgore's demands. I'm so proud of you."

She slowly raised her eyes to meet Gideon's again, comprehension dawning like the first light of day. "It's because of who I am in God's eyes. I'm His. Because He loves me and promised to never leave me, I'm not worthless."

Gideon pulled her hands across the small table and drew her fingers up to his lips. "You are God's treasure." He placed a gentle kiss on each of her hands.

Miss Pearl tiptoed to the back door. " 'Scuse me, I'm just going to go take the laundry off the line." She slipped out, leaving Gideon and Tessa alone.

Gideon rose from his chair and stood with his back to her, looking out the window. "Tessa, I know how you feel about my selling the mercantile and starting a horse ranch. It's been my dream for a long time. I've put a great deal of study into it, and I believe I have God's approval. It will take some time. I need to purchase some acreage, acquire breeding stock, put up fences, a brood mare barn"—he turned to face her—"and a house." He stared at the floor. One boot scuffed the other.

Sorrow pinched her. She'd intended to apologize to him for her hasty opinion, but with everything that had happened, her apology slipped through the cracks. "Gideon, I—"

"Tessa, do you think—"

She smiled. "You first."

Gideon didn't smile. He raised his eyes and held her gaze.

She couldn't look away even if she'd wanted to.

"Tessa, I'd like to ask you to reconsider your opinion."

Emotion swelled in her chest. She wasn't sure she could contain it. He wasn't just asking her to change her mind. He was telling her he valued her support of his dream. "Gideon, you and your father built a solid, reputable business through hard work and integrity. When your father passed away, he left you a legacy. But I see now that the legacy he left isn't the mercantile. It's the integrity he taught you. Your dream will succeed because of that integrity and hard work, but most of all because you have God's blessing."

A light from within slowly lit Gideon's face. "Tessa, there's one more thing I need for God's blessing to be fulfilled." He crossed the kitchen and lowered himself to one knee in front of her. Enfolding her hand in his, he spoke as solemnly as if taking a vow. "Tessa, I love you. My dream won't be complete unless you'll marry me."

A single tear slipped down her cheek. "Gideon, it's my dream, too. Yes, I'll marry you."

He rose and drew her up from the chair. Cupping her face in his hands, he leaned down and sealed their pledge with the gentlest of kisses.

She snuggled into his embrace, releasing the shackles of her father's accusations.

Gideon lifted her chin. "There's just one other question I need to ask you."

She couldn't imagine anything else being important enough to need an answer this minute, but she nodded. "What is it?"

He pressed his lips into a thin line and took a deep breath.

"You said you've already made plans to attend the barn dance with someone." His dark eyes searched her face. "Who?"

Tessa threw her head back and gave free expression to the joy that overflowed within her. "Gideon, it's you. I always planned to go with you. I was just waiting for you to ask me."

epilogue

Willow Creek, Iowa, 1883

Gideon wiped his hands on a rag and tiptoed out of the stall to stand beside his wife. If there was any doubt of God's blessing on his dream, the twin foals standing on wobbly legs beside their mother erased it.

Tessa leaned against him. "Just look at them, Gideon," she whispered. "Aren't they precious? Did you know she was going to have twins?"

Gideon grinned. "Well, I thought she was a might plump, even for a pregnant lady."

His wife lifted her shoulders in a contented sigh. "I'm so glad I got to help bring those little ones into the world."

He slipped his arm around her as they made their way out of the barn to give the new family some privacy. "The two yearlings are coming along well. They're both broken to halter, and by this time next year, I'll start training them to harness."

A high-pitched whinny drew their attention to the small corral attached to the barn where another new mother with her month-old foal trotted along the fence. Beyond the fence, two more mares and their foals grazed in the meadow among the wildflowers.

Gideon paused to lean on the top rail and appreciate the blessings God had given him. "Five strong, healthy foals so far."

Tessa propped her arms on the fence beside him. "The miracle of birth is something I'll never tire of watching."

He grinned down at her and drew her close as they walked toward the house. "If God keeps blessing us like this, we're going to have to add on to the brood mare barn next year."

She cocked her head to one side but kept looking straight ahead. "I think we should add onto the house first."

When he cast a sideways glance at her and saw a twitch play at the corner of her mouth, he thought she was teasing. She'd not made mention before of the house being too small. In fact, she'd told him it was the most beautiful house she'd ever seen.

"Why would we need to add onto the house?"

She peered up at him in a demure fashion. "Think about it. You'll figure it out." She continued on toward the house, leaving him standing by the birch trees, scratching his head.

He watched as she stopped by the vegetable garden to pull a couple of weeds from the row of carrots. *I'll figure it out?*

She dusted off her hands and climbed the front porch step to their home, pausing in the doorway to send him a secretive smile.

Realization dawned, and he let out a whoop of exultation. "Tessa!" He ran and scooped her into his arms, his joyful laughter blending with hers as he twirled her in a crazy circle. When he let her slip to the ground, his arms surrounded her, and he lowered his face to smother her with kisses. God had blessed them with such an amazing love.

A Letter To Our Readers

Dear Reader:

In order that we might better contribute to your reading enjoyment, we would appreciate your taking a few minutes to respond to the following questions. We welcome your comments and read each form and letter we receive. When completed, please return to the following:

Fiction Editor
Heartsong Presents
PO Box 719
Uhrichsville, Ohio 44683

1. Did you enjoy reading *Leave Me Never* by Connie Stevens?
   ❏ Very much! I would like to see more books by this author!
   ❏ Moderately. I would have enjoyed it more if

   _____

   _____

   _____

2. Are you a member of **Heartsong Presents**? ❏ Yes ❏ No
   If no, where did you purchase this book? _____

   _____

3. How would you rate, on a scale from 1 (poor) to 5 (superior), the cover design? _____

4. On a scale from 1 (poor) to 10 (superior), please rate the following elements.

   ____ Heroine   ____ Plot
   ____ Hero   ____ Inspirational theme
   ____ Setting   ____ Secondary characters

5. These characters were special because? _____

_____

_____

6. How has this book inspired your life? _____

_____

_____

7. What settings would you like to see covered in future
   Heartsong Presents books? _____

_____

_____

8. What are some inspirational themes you would like to see
   treated in future books? _____

_____

_____

9. Would you be interested in reading other **Heartsong
   Presents** titles? ❑ Yes ❑ No

10. Please check your age range:
    ❑ Under 18   ❑ 18-24
    ❑ 25-34   ❑ 35-45
    ❑ 46-55   ❑ Over 55

Name _____

Occupation _____

Address _____

City, State, Zip _____

E-mail _____

MICHIGAN BRIDES

The couples in the industrial era must rethink their views of a rapidly changing world before the doors to love can be opened.

Historical, paperback, 352 pages, 5.1875" x 8"

_____

Heart♥ng

Any 6
Heartsong
Presents titles
for only
$20.95*

GET MORE FOR LESS FROM YOUR HISTORICAL ROMANCE!

Buy any assortment of six *Heartsong Presents* titles and save 25% off the already discounted price of $3.99 each!

*plus $4.00 shipping and handling per order and sales tax where applicable. If outside the U.S. please call 740-922-7280 for shipping charges.

HEARTSONG PRESENTS TITLES AVAILABLE NOW:

Presents